ALSO BY RODMAN PHILBRICK

Freak the Mighty

The Fire Pony

Max the Mighty

REM World

The Last Book in the Universe

The Young Man and the Sea

The Mostly True Adventures of Homer P. Figg

Zane and the Hurricane

The Big Dark

WHO KILLED DARIUS DRAKE?

WHO KILLED DARIUS DRAKE?

A MYSTERY BY
RODMAN PHILBRICK

THE BLUE SKY PRESS

An Imprint of Scholastic Inc.
New York

THE BLUE SKY PRESS

Copyright © 2017 by Rodman Philbrick

Library of Congress catalog card number: 2016052083

ISBN 978-0-545-78978-3

10 9 8 7 6 5 4 3 2 1   17 18 19 20 21

Printed in the U.S.A.   23
First edition, October 2017

Book design by Elizabeth Parisi

To Bonnie Verburg, for always pointing me in the right direction, and for lending me her service dog

CHAPTER ONE

Bad Things
Will Happen

WHATEVER YOU'VE HEARD about Darius Drake is probably wrong. Dead wrong. Some of the stories are lies, some are mistaken, and the rest were invented by Darius himself, to fool his enemies.

Enemies. Not school bullies, or mean kids that hated him, although there were plenty of those. I'm talking about real, grown-up enemies who wanted to steal the long-lost treasure Darius recovered and erase him from the world.

I know because I was his only friend.

Not that it started out that way. As far as I was concerned he was just another weirdo. This tall, skinny kid, all arms and legs, shooting up his hand at every opportunity, answering questions before the teacher even thought to ask them. Seemed like maybe he was sneering at those of us who didn't know the answers. Plus he had thick reddish hair that kind of exploded from the top of his head, like an eruption from a hair volcano. Ugh. Girls saw him and rolled their eyes. The boys ignored him, if possible, and dissed him when necessary, to keep their distance. No one wanted to be seen in the vicinity of Darius Drake, and if he wouldn't keep his distance, you persuaded some big, fat, scary-looking dude to back him off.

That would be me. Arthur Bash, thug-for-hire. Hand me a candy bar and point me in the right direction. In this case the end of a crowded cafeteria table where Darius had parked himself for lunch.

"Hey," I say, looming over him. "Beat it."

"Excuse me?"

"Sit somewhere else. This table is taken."

"Ah," he says, raising his chin. "And if I don't?"

"Bad things will happen."

He stands up, slump-shouldered, clutching his tray of gluey mac and cheese. "Any suggestions?"

"Huh?"

"Where I might dine undisturbed."

I shrug, then point. "Over there. Empty table."

He nods like a bobblehead doll and heads for the empty table.

I lower my bulk into the seat he's vacated and inhale the Snickers bar in one fat bite.

Mission accomplished.

CHAPTER TWO

Not Yet Dead

THEY SAY NEVER judge a book by its cover. That applies to me, too. I'm average height, but wide and strong and tough-looking. See me lumbering down the sidewalk with a scowl on my pudgy face, you might be inclined to cross the street. Many do.

If only they knew. A long time ago I learned that if you show fear around here you're dead meat. So I make myself look mean and dangerous by scrunching my bushy eyebrows together and scowling. Grr. Sometimes I practice in a mirror and scare myself. Anyhow, kids started giving me candy bars when they wanted somebody frightened, and I'm always hungry, so I usually go along with it.

As a matter of fact I'm thinking about food the next time Darius Drake crosses my path. I'm heading home after school, trying to remember if there's chocolate chip ice cream in the freezer or if I ate it the night before, when

Darius appears out of nowhere. And he's waving a candy bar like a conductor waving a baton at a really hungry orchestra.

"Arthur Bash," he says. "They say you're the toughest boy in school. You certainly look the part. Strange that I've never actually seen you hit anyone. I'm counting on that, actually."

He watches me track the candy bar with my eyes.

"What do you want?" I say.

"I want you to do what you do. Look menacing. Don't worry, you won't have to fight anybody."

"I'm not worried."

"No? Good. Will three Snickers suffice?"

I hold out my hand.

"One as a down payment, two more upon completion?"

I shrug.

"It's a deal, then," Darius says, placing the candy bar in my fist. "You know the abandoned house on Rutgers Road?"

"That's Stomper territory. Sketchy stuff happens in Stomper."

"Not a problem," Darius says brightly. "Not for the toughest kid in school."

That's when I know I'm in real trouble.

The Anthony J. Stompanado Housing Complex is named after some dead guy that used to be mayor of our little city, Dunbar Mills. If he knew what they made of his name he'd probably roll over in his grave. There are twelve three-story buildings in Stomper, and each building has eight units, so that covers every kind of miserable. There's only one rule in Stomper Land: If you don't live there, don't go there. Strangers are not welcome.

The abandoned house on Rutgers Road isn't officially part of the complex, but it's right on the edge, and everybody knows about the house because it looks so Halloween, with a roof peaked high like a witch's hat, and the windows boarded up, and a saggy old porch melting into the dirt. Supposedly there was a murder there, and that's why the place hasn't been sold or torn down. Half the kids in Dunbar Mills have broken into the place, or bragged they did, or slimed the outside with blood-red graffiti. Not me. I don't believe in witches or ghosts, but as you know by now, I'm not as tough as I look, and one of the things that scares me is rotten floors. What if I fell through the floor and starved to death before they found me?

What an embarrassing way to die.

As we approach the creepy old house, Darius asks, "You scared?"

I shake my head. Throw in an extra scowl to make it convincing.

"I am," he admits. "Could be dangerous. I mean, look at the place."

"So what are we doing here?"

"Observing. Checking numbers."

"Numbers?"

"The street address. There's nothing on the mailbox. Might be something on the front door."

Darius edges up to the porch, squinting. Did I mention he wears glasses? Clunky glasses with thick lenses that make his eyes look like big blue eggs. He studies the peeling paint around the door and then scuttles back to where I'm waiting at the edge of the property.

"Numerical identification confirmed," he says with a tight smile. "This is the place, Ace."

I've no idea what he's talking about until he pulls out a crinkled envelope and shows me the return address. "The street numbers fell off the building or were stolen," he says. "But the marks are still there. 123 Rutgers Road. See? It matches."

The envelope is addressed to Darius Drake, care of the Stonehill Home for Children. He's not the only Stonehill kid in our school, but he's the smartest, and for sure he's the weirdest. There's no name on the return address, just the street number and zip code.

"Nobody lives here, but nevertheless someone used this return address," he points out. "Strange, isn't it?"

"I guess."

"Not as strange as this," Darius says, handing me the letter itself. "Read it."

I unfold the letter. There's only one sentence, scrawled in rusty-brown ink.

Who killed Darius Drake?

"Dude," I say. "You're not dead."

"Not yet," he says.

CHAPTER THREE

A Bloodstained Question

MUST BE A million bricks in the Stonehill Home for Children. It has two fat chimneys rising from a steep slate roof and a bunch of small shiny windows that look like animal eyes. Dark glassy eyes reflecting the huge oak trees that hide the place from the road. Back in the old days it was Stonehill Academy, a private school for the sons of factory owners, and then later it became an orphanage. Not that they're all orphans, at least not technically. Most of the kids in Stonehill have parents or family that can't take care of them. Like in prison or on drugs, or maybe the kids can't be placed in foster homes. Some have serious physical or mental disorders and need special care. Others have what they call temperament issues. Screamers. Biters. And then there's Darius, who gets straight A's but is just too strange to be adopted.

So he says.

I knew about the home—everybody does, all the kids—but this is my first time inside it. No surprise, the place creeps me out a little. Not because it's spooky or scary, nothing like that. It's actually kind of cheerful, in a sad-but-trying way. But it makes me think, what if it was me? What if both my parents died and nobody wanted me? Like that.

Anyhow, the nice lady in reception checks off my name on the visitor list and sends me up to Darius Drake's room. I don't know what I was expecting. Maybe something like a broom closet, or a cupboard under the stairs like Harry Potter. Turns out all the residents have their own bedrooms. Darius's room is bigger than the others because it used to be an old science lab, from when the place had been a school. And Darius has filled the desk and cabinets with all kinds of scientific gizmos. Beakers, test tubes, microscopes, all that mad scientist stuff.

"Mr. Bash," he says, ushering me in. "Welcome to my not-so-humble abode."

"Hey," I say.

He studies me, head cocked slightly to one side, like a bird studying a worm. "I deduce, from your expression, that this is your first visit to the Stonehill Home for Children."

I nod.

"You're tempted to feel pity, perhaps. The poor orphan

boy. Boo-hoo. Well, don't. Erase it from your brain. This is where I belong," he says, pushing his thick glasses up his freckled nose. "My weirdness likes it here."

My weirdness likes it here. I've no idea what he means by that. And I'm not sure I want to know. I'm not interested in a long explanation about how he got here, or boring stuff about the history of the Stonehill Home for Children.

I'm all about the candy bars.

Snickers, specifically. Perfectly chilled in the lab refrigerator.

He hands one to me, unwraps another for himself.

"Written in blood," he says. "The anonymous letter."

"No way."

He holds up a slender test tube. "See the lines of sediment? Human blood. My tests were conclusive as to species. But there are seven billion humans on the planet. In an effort to narrow down the suspect pool, I sent a sample in for DNA testing, but that may take weeks."

My tests were conclusive as to species. I mean, who talks like that? No wonder nerd alarms go off when Darius Drake is in the vicinity.

"I don't get it," I admit. "Why not use a pen or a marker to write the note? Why use blood?"

He shrugs. "I can only speculate. To make a point? Ink could be a joke. Blood you have to take seriously."

"Okay. But what does it have to do with that rotten old house?"

"That's the question, isn't it? Why that particular address?"

For some reason Darius seems really pleased. A blood-stained question. Nothing makes him happier.

CHAPTER FOUR

Meet My Fist

THE NICE LADY at the desk in the lobby smiles at me and Darius as he checks out.

"Destination?"

"Downtown. Might go to the library."

"Very good." She makes an entry in her desk computer. "Enjoy your day."

I wait until we're outside in the long curving driveway before asking, in a low voice, "They let you go, just like that?"

Darius chuckles. "Yeah, they do. I'm a resident, not an inmate. Some of the troubled kids can't leave the grounds except on group trips, but I have privileged status. Also, I never cause trouble, keep my room tidy, talk to the counselor every month, and get straight A's in school. I'm like the ideal resident, except I don't want to leave."

"Why not?"

He gives me a look. "Stonehill may not be normal to you, but it is to me. It's my home."

"Cool."

Darius holds a finger up in the air, as if testing the breeze. "Changed my mind," he announces. "We may go to the library—it's one of my favorite destinations—but first we're making a slight detour."

———

So we go back to that rotten old place. The Halloween house. The wreck with a roof like a witch's hat.

I'm not exactly enthusiastic about the idea. In fact, the closer we get, the less I like it.

"No way," I finally say, halting in my tracks. "This is a truly bad idea."

We're about a block from the Stomper projects, having walked from Stonehill. A mile or so of Darius Drake running off at the mouth about his various scientific accomplishments, which include galvanic reactions in frogs' legs, as well as testing for human blood. Trust me, you don't want to know what a galvanic reaction is, not when it applies to dead frogs.

"Keep your candy bars," I tell him, because I'm getting more and more nervous. "I'm not crossing the line into Stomper territory. For sure I'm not going inside that falling-down house. You can't make me."

"You already ate the candy bars. We have a contract."

"I never signed a contract."

"The first bite was an oral affirmation."

That's Darius trying to be funny, riffing on words. I didn't get it until later, because at the time, when he said it, I was too scared to think straight. There are all kinds of rumors about Stomper, how outsiders have ventured into the complex and vanished without a trace. The scariest stories are about a Stomper resident called Scar Man, who is so ugly that just looking at him makes you go blind. That can't be true, right? But I'd rather not find out, just in case.

"What do you think is in that crummy house, anyhow?" I ask. "A clue? Like one you'll find with a magnifying glass? Only clue will be a fist in the face. Or worse."

"I'm not afraid of hooligans," Darius says cheerfully. "You'll protect me. As per our contract."

Hooligan. Another word that nobody uses. He saunters across the street without looking back, as if convinced I'll follow.

And like an idiot, I do. Not that I have any intention of fighting the locals, or anyone. No way. A Stomper shows his face, I'm out of there.

On our first visit I never got any closer to the creepy old house than the front yard. And Darius only got near enough to see where the street numbers had been before they rusted away or fell off. This time Darius walks right up to the front door and tries ringing the bell. Nothing. He raises a skinny fist and knocks.

The door creaks open.

He steps inside, into the shadows.

My brain is screaming NO WAY, but my stupid feet follow in his path. Up the rotten, creaky steps. Across the rickety porch. Into the same moldy darkness that just swallowed the so-called genius Darius Drake.

Naturally I'm expecting to fall through the floor and into a basement full of skeletons. But the floor seems surprisingly firm under my feet, and when my eyes finally adjust to the dim interior, there's Darius with his hands on his hips and a smug look on his freckled face.

"See? Perfectly safe."

The door slams behind me.

They say fat boys can't jump, but I launch like a booster rocket. If the ceilings weren't so high, I'd have bumped my head.

"Just the wind," Darius says.

Once my heart slows down I start to notice a few things. The place isn't abandoned and stripped bare like I expected. The furniture is old and lumpy but still usable. Lots of little tables piled high with magazines, and bookshelves filled with books, and even an old tube TV.

"Somebody lives here," I say.

"Indeed," Darius says. "Very possibly the person who sent me the letter."

I glance at the closed door uneasily. "They might come back."

Darius shrugs. "Or maybe they never left."

Which nearly makes me jump again. Could the owner of the house be hiding in the next room, ready to pounce? And how come a place that looks so falling-down on the outside seems more or less okay on the inside?

Darius slips his way around the furniture, into the little kitchen. A few dirty dishes in the sink, scummy but dry. He lifts a plate, sniffs it. "Whoever lives here has been gone for a few days."

"I think we should get out of here."

Darius stares at the slightly saggy ceiling. "Is that what prompted the enigmatic letter? A hasty departure?"

"Enig-what-ic? Does that mean 'handwritten'?"

He seems pleased by my confusion. "*Enigmatic*, derived from the Greek, 'to speak in riddles.'"

"Yeah, whatever. I'm out of here."

Stay any longer and Darius'll figure out how scared I really am. Nothing enigmatic about that.

I'm almost to the door when a deep, snarly voice freezes my feet.

"Hey, you!"

A big, barrel-chested man squeezes through the door, filling the little room with his ragged sneer and his dead eyes. His face looks like a skull smiling through a bowl of pudding. And one side of his face looks sort of melted.

Scar Man. He's real.

I want to run, but there's nowhere to go and no place to hide.

"Pleased to meet you," Darius says, offering his skinny hand.

Scar Man growls. "Yeah? Meet my fist."

CHAPTER FIVE

You Can't Argue with a Lunatic

THEY SAY JUST before you die your life flashes before you. Not me. What flashed before me was all the great meals I was going to miss. Double cheeseburgers with extra pickles. Biscuits and gravy. Chicken and gravy. Anything and gravy. Salty snacks. Ice cream. Candy. Everything that was good in my life, ended by a sneering Stomper who wanted to hammer me into the floor like a big, fat nail.

Scar Man grabs Darius by the scruff of the neck and aims his other fist at my head, ready to pound a two-for-one beating into us. Then for some reason he hesitates and lets Darius go. "Huh. You ain't but kids," he says, as if surprised. "Why are you breaking into this place?"

"The door was unlocked."

The man with the melted face stares at Darius like he's a bug that needs squashing. "Yeah? Don't matter. Nobody allowed inside less they invited."

"But I was invited," Darius says, holding up the envelope. "Someone sent me a letter mailed from this address."

The big man shrugs like he couldn't care less, but his small, close-set eyes spark with interest. "What's it say, this letter?"

"I'd prefer to discuss that with whoever sent the letter. Unless it was you."

"Me? I ain't sent no letter."

"Do you live here? Is this your place?"

The big man shakes his head. "The dude lives here took sick. I'm keeping an eye out while he's gone."

"The owner has been hospitalized?"

"None of your business. He's away for now. Maybe he get better; maybe he don't. Only thing you need to know, he ain't here and you're trespassing on private property."

Darius remains defiant. "What I 'need to know' is the owner's name and his location. Someone has threatened my life and I have a right to know who and why."

The man with the melted face hesitates, as if he can't believe this skinny, red-haired kid won't take no for an answer. A vein throbs on the side of his thick neck.

"Get out of here," he says, in a voice that's almost a growl. "Leave this place and don't come back. I won't say it again."

I may not be a genius, but I can tell when someone the size of a small planet is about to resort to violence. So before Darius Drake gets us killed, I wrap an arm around his skinny chest and yank him out of that house and away from the man with the melted face.

"Let me go!" Darius protests, trying to wriggle free. "You are in my employ!"

"I quit."

"Then release me! I'll go back on my own!"

No point arguing. You can't argue with a lunatic. All you can do is drag him home.

CHAPTER SIX

What Selma Saw

I'M DONE WORKING for Darius Drake. He's too strange and out of control. He may be some kind of genius, but standing up to a local legend like Scar Man? That's just plain stupid.

When I finally escort him back to Stonehill—possibly saving his stupid life—he's mad enough to spit. So mad he won't look me in the eye as I shove him up the stairs and into that mad scientist room of his, hoping the staff won't see us, which they don't.

"How dare you! You had no business intervening in a personal matter!"

I shrug. "Did you happen to notice his prison tattoos? They say Scar Man did time for murder. They say he makes people disappear, especially kids."

Darius snorts. "Don't be ridiculous. Those are just ugly rumors based on his disfigurement."

"Think about it. Maybe it was Scar Man who sent you the letter, written in his own blood. Maybe you were going to be his next victim. Sorry, but I wasn't about to stick around and find out."

"You have no idea what's really going on! Not a clue!"

"You're right. And I intend to keep it that way."

He's still ranting when I leave.

———

When my parents divorced, Mom got the house, a little two-bedroom ranch in Dunbar Acres, which is sort of run-down, but nothing like Stomper, that's for sure. Mom never talks about what happened between her and Dad, but I know it still makes her mad. And sad, too. The weird thing is they both work in the same hospital, so they see each other all the time, like it or not. Mom is a nurse; Dad is an X-ray technician, and—get this—his new wife is a heart surgeon in the very same hospital. So Mom is stuck seeing her all the time, too.

Talk about Suckville. I'd hate that, having to be polite to someone who hurt me, even if I really, really needed the job. But what do I know? And to be honest, Dad's new wife is always real polite and kind when I stay over one night a week. *Learning how the other half lives*, is how my mother puts it, because the new wife earns lots of money, even if Dad doesn't make that much himself, after he pays child support, which they argue about all the time.

Anyhow, Mom is on night shift this week, so she's around when I get home. Napping on the sofa in her ER scrubs, which means she hasn't really gone to bed yet, even though she's dead tired. And when I try to sneak through to the kitchen she pops up. Looking guilty, as if napping in the afternoon is something to be ashamed of.

"Arthur, sweetie! Are you okay? I was expecting you earlier. Is everything okay?"

"Everything is fine, Mom. Go back to sleep."

She fights a yawn. "In a minute. I wanted to ask you something about your new friend."

"I don't have a new friend, Mom."

"The tall, skinny boy with the red hair. Selma saw you guys over near the Stompanado projects."

Selma is Mom's best friend. They work together in the ER. Selma is nice, but she's one of those grown-ups who notice what kids are up to, and that can be a problem.

"She was on her way home and waved, but I guess you didn't see her."

"I didn't, no. Sorry."

"Huh," Mom says, not surprised that her son failed to notice someone waving at him. "Thing is, Selma knows that boy with the red hair. She works a volunteer shift at Stonehill twice a month."

I nod glumly. Thinking, *Here it comes*, a warning to stay away, when I've already decided to do that on my own.

"The Drake boy," Mom says. "His parents died in a car wreck when he was little. Did you know that?"

I shake my head.

"Selma says he's very bright and well-behaved, but outside of the staff he hasn't got a friend in the world. Or didn't until he met you."

I raise both hands, making a back-off gesture. "We're not friends, okay? I was just, um, doing him a favor. Helping him out."

Mom smiles.

"No, really," I insist. "We're. Not. Friends. Not even close!"

"I think it's great," she says. "But I worry about you being so close to the projects. Most of those Stomper folks are just folks who happen to be poor. But some, well, I'd rather you didn't play near there."

"We weren't playing, Mom."

"Of course you weren't. I just want you to be careful. Never go near that neighborhood alone. And never after dark. Okay?"

"Okay."

Then Mom smiles through a big yawn and goes to her room.

CHAPTER SEVEN

Bash Man

NEXT DAY DARIUS DRAKE is a no-show at school. Probably scared to show his face in public. Or unwilling to hear the stupid rumors about our encounter with Scar Man. Rumors that couldn't be more messed up.

"Dude," one of the cool kids says, stopping me in the hall on the way to homeroom. "That's really awesome what you did. Stomped on Vinnie Meeks!"

"Who?" I manage to say.

"Vincent Meeks. The Scar Man himself. Heard you beat the ugly sucker to a pulp. Way to go, Bash Man!"

The kid high-fives me before it really hits home, what he's saying. It's totally insane, the idea that I'd beaten up a full-grown man. Insane and probably dangerous, because what if Scar Man heard I was bragging on him? He'd twist me like a fat cruller, until my brains oozed out my ears.

I should deny it, explain that my encounter had been exactly the opposite of winning. But I can't find the words—or maybe part of me kind of enjoys being called Bash Man—and by the time lunch block comes around I'm like this celebrity or something. Kids who yesterday treated me like a total loser are suddenly acting like we've always been tight. Oh, I know it isn't real, but it's fun pretending to be popular, or at least famous.

At the time, I don't think too much about who might have started the rumors. Mom's friend Selma had seen me in the area and I hadn't noticed, so it could have been anybody. Kids that lived in Stompanado housing who maybe wanted to take Scar Man down a peg.

Doesn't really matter. It's out of my hands. All I can do is enjoy being king of the cafeteria while it lasts.

Which isn't that long, as it turns out.

———

I'm heading home, taking my time—this is maybe the first time I've ever wanted school not to end—when this straggly street dude in a soiled hoodie staggers onto the sidewalk and almost knocks me down. He smells like a garbage pail, which is probably where he found his last meal, and he's so covered with dirt you can't tell what color he is under all that crud.

"Eww! Dude, I'm sorry, but you stink."

"I should hope so," the street dude says. "That was my intention. An obnoxious odor is often the best disguise. No one bothers to look closely if their eyes are watering."

"Darius?"

He takes a bow.

"Are you crazy?" I ask.

"As a fox," he says, pleased with himself. "Appearing homeless is like being invisible. Nobody wants to look at you. It's as if you don't exist. Therefore I am able to observe and overhear. And I heard interesting things about you. Very interesting."

My brain is telling me to stop right here. Explain that I no longer work for him, not for any amount of Snickers bars, but all I can manage is to sputter something about the bogus rumors that are spreading through the school like poison ivy.

"Bash Man?" he says, nodding happily. "So they really called you that? Excellent! That may prove useful, as an intimidating factor. As to the rest, it went exactly as planned."

"What are you talking about?"

He steps off the sidewalk, into the bushes, and emerges with a backpack. "Change of costume," he explains. From a small zippered pocket in the backpack he produces a cheap-looking cell phone. "The rumors originated with me, of course. Posted shortly after dawn to a site frequented by the cool kids. And as intended, it went locally viral."

He sheds the smelly hoodie and pulls on a fresh sweatshirt. Then scrubs his face clean with some Handi Wipes. I'm standing there shaking my head because, as smart as he is, Darius Drake doesn't seem to get it.

Finally I manage to get the words together. "He'll be coming for us. We're as good as dead."

"Ah," he says. "I assume you refer to Vincent Meeks, aka Scar Man? Put your mind at ease. I'll handle Scar Man. In any case the message wasn't for him. It was for the mystery man."

"Mystery man?" I say, confused.

"The man who recently lived in the house on Rutgers Road, remember? The man who might have sent me the letter, likely written in his own blood. Call him Mystery Man for lack of a known identity. Scar Man won't reveal Mystery Man's name or his specific location, so I devised this scheme to bring us to his attention, thereby increasing the likelihood that he'll attempt to contact me again."

I stare at him, shaking my head. "No doubt about it. You are totally insane."

"On the contrary, my actions have been completely

logical. You will come to understand the wisdom of my plan. Unless, of course, it turns out that I've been mistaken. But even then you'll have nothing to fear."

"Why is that?"

He shrugs and says, "Because we'll both be dead."

CHAPTER EIGHT

Cupcake Sad

IT'S NONE OF your business exactly what happened when my parents got divorced. All you need to know is that when I was ten, Dad moved out and married this really well-off doctor and is helping her raise her perfect daughter from *her* first marriage. Oh, and when I spend one night a week at my dad's new home, it's way on the other side of town. The upscale side. It has a swimming pool and a tennis court. And a built-in freezer full of hamburgers and ice cream that nobody eats but me, because my dad and his new family are all so thin and perfect.

As usual I'm sort of hiding in a corner of the kitchen, wolfing down microwaved burgers and double-chocolate cupcakes, when Deirdre strolls in wearing her tennis whites. Deirdre is a year ahead of me in school. We're not at the same school because my grades are average and that won't do for an exclusive private school.

Not a surprise we'd be in different schools because she occupies a totally different planet.

Don't get me wrong, she's not a bad person, and not nearly as snobby as you might assume, being so rich and beautiful. And she's never been not nice to me, not on purpose.

Anyhow, she notices me wedged into the breakfast nook and grins and says, "Hey there."

After pouring herself a skinny glass of bottled water she slips into the opposite side of the booth and watches me inhaling cupcakes. "Can I ask you a question, Arthur?"

My mouth is jammed full but I manage to nod.

"Mommy says you eat to make up for a sad childhood. Are you sad, Arthur?"

She's not trying to be mean, she really wants to know. Deirdre is like that, curious about everyone. Like if she keeps asking questions eventually everything will make sense.

"I'm just fat," I tell her. "And hungry. Always hungry. Want one?"

I push the plate of cupcakes over to her side of the table.

"Okay," she says, and takes one. Holding it like you might hold a dead mouse you found in your sock drawer. She pretends to nibble the frosting, then returns it to the plate and pats her lips clean with a cloth napkin. "I heard you have a new friend. That's nice. Friends are essential."

"That's so not true."

"That friends are essential?"

"That I have one. Darius Drake hired me to help him check out some stupid old house, that's all. And I already quit."

"What house?"

I tell her about the house at 123 Rutgers Road. And then I tell her pretty much everything, including the letter written in blood that asked the question "Who killed Darius Drake?" and how it didn't make any sense because nobody had killed him. Not yet.

She stares at me, her eyes gleaming so bright and true it's amazing I don't melt into a puddle of blubber. "Fascinating," she says, meaning it. "Now, what do you mean he 'hired' you?"

Here's where I should excuse myself and go away, but instead I find myself telling her about pretending to be a tough guy for candy bars. A thug-for-hire.

She shakes her head, amazed. "But, Arthur, you're not a thug. You're sweet and sometimes you're a little sad. A big, strong teddy bear. Not a tough guy at all."

"Yeah? How about this?"

I put on my meanest face and glare at her.

She laughs. "Really? Kids fall for that?"

"Everybody but you."

She thinks about it. "I worry you might get hurt, pretending to be someone you're not. If somebody takes you up on it, I mean."

"I worry, too. But I'd rather kids felt scared of me than sorry for me, you know? I don't like it when you say I'm sad."

She sighs, which naturally makes her look even more beautiful.

"Arthur, being sad is not a crime. And I don't care if you're fat. Truly, I don't. People come in all sizes. I just want you to be happy."

So that's my stepsister, Deirdre. Sometimes I wish she wasn't so perfect. If she wasn't so perfect maybe she wouldn't feel sorry for me.

Thinking about that makes me hungry, so after she says good-bye and glides out of the kitchen I get to work on another plate of cupcakes.

"Arthur?"

She leans back into the room, catches me with my mouth stuffed.

"I was thinking about your friend. You know his parents died in a car crash one night? He was like, I don't know, three years old or something when it happened? He was in the car, Arthur. What I heard, his heart stopped beating. So technically . . . he was dead. They shocked him back to life. He survived but had to be revived. Do you understand?"

"Yeah," I say, dumbfounded. "You're saying the answer to 'Who killed Darius Drake?' might be about what happened to him the night his parents died."

"See, Arthur? You think you're not smart, but you are."

CHAPTER NINE

The Secret in the Stacks

THE NEXT MORNING I get called into the principal's office. I figure they heard about Bash Man going viral and wanted to set me straight or maybe even boot me out of school. But when I get there it's even worse than I expected.

Darius Drake is kicking back in a visitor's chair, a triumphant smile splitting his freckled face, and Ms. Bamberger, the principal, is beaming at me like I've won some kind of prize.

"Arthur, I am so pleased to hear that you have taken the initiative. This is splendid news! Splendid!"

"Um, thanks, I guess."

"We always knew you had potential, Arthur, if only you would apply yourself. Naturally there will be paperwork to sign, but parental permission has already been granted—as soon as Darius came to me with the request for an independent project investigating the history of the public housing projects, I contacted your mother. Once I explained, she expressed enthusiasm for the idea."

The idea, as explained by Principal Bamberger, is an advanced placement project in which Darius and I will be allowed off campus to conduct research at the nearby city hall and public library complex. Words like *data* and *statistics* make me wince, but she doesn't seem to notice. In the end I mumble and nod my way through the interview without saying much of anything, which makes sense because I don't have a clue what Darius is really up to.

Next thing I know we're outside the main entrance, waving bye-bye to the security guard. Free to go. On a school day! Excused from class to "pursue research in the public sector for advanced placement activity."

"Dude," I say. "Am I dreaming? What does that even mean?"

Darius grins, highly pleased with himself. "It means Ms. Bamberger hopes that your association with me will improve your academic standing. Also, educators love it when students reach out to the community. I knew all that, of course, and simply provided what she wanted to hear."

"You made it up?"

"No, no. Not exactly," he says. "For instance we really are headed to the city hall archives, where we shall, with any luck, solve an actual mystery."

He strides off without a backward glance, as if fully expecting that I'll follow in his footsteps. And like a moron, I do.

———

You might expect the clerk at the city desk to blow us off. A couple of kids on a school project? Forget about it. But much to my surprise, the clerk, Mrs. Ferrini, is really helpful and nice, and she tells us how to get to the Registry of Deeds so we can do our research. Then she gives me a look like she's got tape measures and scales inside her head, and she's measuring me up. "You're quite sturdy for your age, young man. I suppose you play sports?"

"Um, not really."

"Well, don't be surprised if my husband attempts to recruit you one of these days. He's the varsity football coach."

I nod and try to look happy, but the idea of going out for football makes me feel a little sick. It wouldn't take them long to figure out what a big fat coward I really am.

As we head down to the Registry of Deeds, Darius says, "You'll notice she didn't suggest *I* should play sports."

"Do you want to?"

He laughs. "Not in the least. Smelly locker rooms? Towel snapping? I think not. My talents lie elsewhere."

In the lower level of the registry, in the cool dimness of a big basement area, we find a place they call "the stacks." Probably because there are stacks and stacks of books on metal shelves. Large books made up of bound maps, covering every inch of land in the county. Those are the map books. The deed books are smaller but thicker, and so heavy it takes the two of us to lift one onto the reading desk.

The air smells of leather and old books. I must be some kind of weirdo, because to me that's a good smell.

Anyhow, we get to work finding the deed books that interest Darius and pulling them from the shelves. To be honest, I'm not sure what a deed is or why we should care about them. Darius explains: "Each time a piece of property changes hands, a new deed is issued and entered into these ledgers. I want to find the deed that shows who owns 123 Rutgers Road. I want to know if the owner sent me that letter written in blood, and if so, why. Maybe his identity is right here," he says, tapping a skinny finger on the stack of deed books.

"Huh. So you're thinking Mystery Man not only lived at the house, he's also the registered owner?"

"Quite possibly. There's only one way to find out."

First we find 123 Rutgers Road on the land map—easier said than done, but we do finally locate it—and then we start flipping pages in the deed books until we get a match.

What we find, neatly typed and pasted into the book, is so shocking that for once in his life Darius Drake is at a loss for words. He doesn't have to speak, because his name is right there on the page:

Pop Pop LLC in Trust for Darius Edgar Drake

"Dude," I finally say. "Does that mean *you* own the house?"

CHAPTER TEN

Hiding in Plain Sight

YEAH, OKAY, I intended to quit working for Darius. And I really meant it, too. Until he found a cool way to get us out of school for the day, so of course I went along. Who wouldn't? And I admit it was exciting when we found his name on the deed for that spooky old house because it raised so many other questions that my brain was spinning like a hoverboard with a blown battery.

But I never, ever intended to go back to that house. No way. Didn't matter whose name was on the deed, it was still Stomper territory, and I'm afraid of Scar Man because, well, because I'm not crazy. You'd have to be insane not to be afraid of a human bulldozer, right? Which means Darius Drake is certifiably insane. And maybe me, too, for going along with him.

"Be assured we are in no danger. According to my

calculations there's a ninety-three percent chance that Scar Man will cooperate."

It's the next day after school. I'm supposed to be on my way home, but somehow I'm sitting on the steps of the house at 123 Rutgers Road. I'm hoping Selma isn't going to drive past and tell my mom. We're waiting for a known criminal to deliver us the keys.

Really? I mean, what are the chances? Just because Darius managed to call the lawyer for something called Pop Pop LLC, which is holding the property in trust for him until he's an adult? The lawyer refused to discuss the identity of the trust holder. That was confidential, and protected by the lawyer-client privilege, but he agreed to contact Scar Man and inform him that Darius had a right to inspect the property that would one day be his.

"Pop Pop LLC," I say. "Sounds like a hip-hop producer."

"LLC is 'limited liability corporation.' Sort of like 'incorporated' but more private. Who it truly represents remains a mystery."

"*Pop pop.* The sound of gunfire. Last sound we hear."

Darius chuckles. "Have a little faith, Bash Man."

I'm keeping a sharp eye on the street in the vicinity of the Stompanado projects, figuring that's where Scar Man will appear. Catch sight of him first and maybe I'll have time to grab Darius by his scrawny neck and drag him away before the big man reduces us to ground hamburger.

But as usual I'm focusing on the wrong thing, because it turns out he's already here. Inside the house. Probably listening to every word we say. My heart just about stops when the lock clicks and the door creaks open and suddenly he's looming over us like some sort of human tornado.

"This a bad idea," he says in his raspy, swallowed-a-bucket-of-nails voice.

I couldn't agree more.

"You spoke to the owner?" Darius asks.

"If you call him that. Told you, that crazy old man is out of it."

"What's his name? His current location? Who is he?"

The big man sighs. "You find out soon enough. He knows who *you* are, that's all that matters."

Scar Man opens his massive fist. In his callused palm is a shiny new house key.

He hands the key to Darius and leaves, muttering to himself.

————

First thing Darius does when we get inside is settle down on the recliner. He looks around like the chair is his new throne and this is his kingdom. Which in a way maybe it is.

"I still don't get it. Why would someone you don't know leave you a house?"

"That's what we're here to find out."

We decide to search for a safe. We check behind some old paintings on the wall. Roll back the rugs to see if maybe there's a floor safe, or at least some loose boards. Nothing.

I open every drawer in the kitchen. Nothing but the usual utensils, including a hand-crank eggbeater so old it probably arrived with the Pilgrims. Nothing in the cupboards but a few plates and bowls and a coffee mug from the 1964 World's Fair.

I even check in the oven. Nothing but cobwebs and dust.

"Doesn't look like he used the kitchen much," I say.

Darius has stopped searching and has taken a seat in the small living room. His eyes are red and watery from all the dust, but he doesn't seem to care. Nothing matters but solving the mystery. "If I were Mystery Man, where would I hide my secrets?" he says. "Not in a safe, because safes can be cracked or carted away. File cabinet? Too obvious. Computer file? There seems to be no computer. No tablets or cells, no devices of any kind. I don't even see evidence of a landline phone."

"He was off the grid."

"Certainly appears that way," Darius says with grudging agreement. "So where did he hide stuff?"

"Inside the walls?"

He shakes his head. "Too hard to retrieve. No, if I was living in a place like this, and I required the protection of someone like Scar Man, there's only one place."

"We already checked for loose floorboards," I point out.

"In plain sight," he says, rising from his throne.

He goes to one of the crowded bookshelves, picks out a book, and begins leafing through the pages. "What does this place have the most of? Books. And what are thieves least likely to steal? Books."

I shrug and pull out a dusty book and flip it open. Page through it. Put it back, pick up another. The third book I pick up opens on an old photograph, which flutters to the floor. The faded image shows a dorky-looking guy with a ponytail and a big grin, holding hands with a little girl with a similar smile.

I hand it to Darius. "Father and daughter?"

He studies it. "Quite possibly," he says, then tucks the photo into his shirt pocket.

"We could quit, come back another day."

"No way. Let's do this."

Over the next hour we find about two dozen photographs hidden in the books. The same dorky guy and the same girl are in many of the pictures, in various combinations with other people, including someone who looks like the girl's mother. It's as if a family album was taken apart and scattered among the books. But there are no names on the pictures, and no way to know whose family it is, although I'm voting for Mystery Man, whoever he is.

I mean, who else can it be?

I mention my theory to Darius, but he just shrugs and keeps searching through the books, so I go back to doing the same thing. And I find something, too. Not a photograph. A small, yellowed newspaper article clipped out and used as a bookmark. Or maybe, as Darius had suggested, to hide in plain sight.

"Huh," I say, scanning the clipping. "The Dunbar diamonds."

Darius is suddenly beside me, craning to see the article. "What?"

"The Dunbar diamonds. They've never been found."

It's obvious from the puzzled and irritated look on his face that Darius hasn't got a clue.

Wow. I know something a genius doesn't.

CHAPTER ELEVEN

What Pop Pop Means

THE DUNBAR DIAMONDS are a local legend from almost a hundred years ago. I first heard about them in fourth grade when one of the kids in my class gave a report called "Interesting Facts About Our City." Supposedly Donald Dunbar, the owner of Dunbar Mills—the factory, not the city—had a million-dollar diamond necklace made for the young woman he loved, but she died before he could give it to her. It was like this sappy, sad love story, where a zillionaire businessman falls for a beautiful brainy girl and she dies tragically, ruining the rest of his life. He never sold the necklace, but years later, when he finally croaked, it was nowhere to be found. Some think it was stolen, others that it remains hidden where the mill owner left it. Possibly in a grave. Others say it never really existed, that the Dunbar diamonds are no more real than a unicorn. Nobody knows anything for sure, so people are free to believe what they want to believe.

Which is pretty much what the newspaper clipping says, before announcing a "new development in the case."

AMATEUR ARCHAEOLOGIST AND PART-TIME TREA-sure hunter Winston Brooks has announced a joint venture with financial mogul Jasper Jones, in search of the famed Dunbar diamonds.

"I have developed a new line of inquiry that we feel confident will lead us to the necklace," said Brooks. "Mr. Jones is providing financial backing and manpower. I will be in charge of the research. And to those who doubt the necklace still exists, let me remind them of one fact we can all agree on: Diamonds are forever."

Based on photographs taken when the necklace was originally created, and documentation from the original jeweler, experts estimate that the Dunbar diamonds might currently be worth as much as fifteen million dollars . . . if, as Mr. Brooks suggests, they still exist.

After reading the article and muttering to himself, Darius holds the yellowed paper up to the light and examines it from every angle.

"The age of the paper can easily be confirmed in the

lab, but my preliminary conclusion is that this appears to be genuine."

"It's just an old clipping, probably used to mark a page. Why would it be fake?"

Darius lowers the piece of newspaper and studies me instead, as if deciding whether or not he should share something. Eventually he says, "Because he was known to fake documents."

"Who?"

Darius looks away. "The amateur archaeologist, Winston Brooks. He went to prison for forgery, financial fraud, and tax evasion. I knew that before we started. I assumed he had forged checks and failed to pay his taxes, but if this article is correct, it seems likely that his crime had something to do with the search for a long-lost necklace."

Something about the way he speaks, his flat, unemotional tone, gives me a sinking feeling. "Dude, why do you already know about this guy going to jail?"

Darius has no expression on his face. No know-it-all smirk, no smile or frown. Nothing.

"Because according to my birth certificate, my mother was Eleanor Brooks, later Eleanor Drake when she got married," he says. "Winston Brooks was her father. Therefore he's my maternal grandfather. And given the photos we found, and this clipping, it's probable that he's our Mystery

Man—the man who until recently lived here, and who quite possibly sent me that letter written in blood."

Now it's my turn to sink into the creaky old easy chair.

"Whoa. You knew this when you hired me?"

He stares at the floor. "Some. At the time it was more like a guess, that the letter might have had something to do with what happened when my parents died. Then we discovered this house was left to me. Whoever asked the question 'Who killed Darius Drake?' wanted me to put it all together, to figure it out."

"You think it could be about the accident? The one that killed your parents?"

"Maybe."

Without really thinking about it I blurt out, "I heard you died, too. That your heart stopped beating."

His head whips around and suddenly he's staring at me, his eyes enormous behind the thick lenses. "Where did you hear that?" he demands.

"I have a sister who knows everything. Deirdre. My stepsister."

He goes back to staring at the wall. He's embarrassed, and I'm embarrassed, too. Because I know what it's like, having people talk about me behind my back. What names they call me. Arty Farty. Biscuit Butt. Even Bash Man, which sounds cool but isn't if you think about it. Whatever they call me, one thing is certain: They're all really glad they're not Arthur Bash, the fat whale who scares kids for candy bars.

"What else did she tell you?" he snaps.

"Nothing. But she's one of those girls who knows everybody's business. She doesn't mean any harm by it; she's just curious about everything."

"Evidently," he says in an angry tone.

"Do you care what people think?" I ask.

"No," he says.

"Me neither."

I'm pretty sure we're both lying.

Darius doesn't say much for the rest of the afternoon. We search through all the books and magazines methodically. Leafing through pages, shaking them out. There are no other newspaper clippings, but we find another dozen or so photographs, similarly faded, of the same family. Darius Drake's family; I get that now. The dorky-looking guy with a ponytail must be his grandfather, the one who was sent to prison. I assume the little girl is Darius's mother, although he never exactly says so. The reverent way he handles those old photographs makes me think maybe he's never seen a picture of his mom, at least not from her childhood.

Before leaving we tidy up, returning all the books to the shelves and restacking the magazines.

"Maybe we can come back another day," I suggest. "See

if we can find more evidence. Something to prove this is your grandfather's house."

Darius won't look me in the eye.

"I think I figured it out," he says.

"You did? Figured what out?"

"That name on the deed, what it means. Pop Pop LLC."

"What are you talking about? What haven't you told me?"

Darius stares at the floor again and speaks without expression.

"I don't remember much of anything from before I went to Stonehill. Nothing about my parents. But I do remember a little bit about my grandfather. I think he took care of me after the accident, before he went to jail. And when I looked at these pictures? The guy with the ponytail? I'm pretty sure I called him Pop Pop."

CHAPTER TWELVE

The Red Menace

NORMALLY WHEN I put my head down on the pillow, I'm sound asleep in about two minutes. But after searching that old house and finding out about some crazy treasure hunt for diamonds that might not even exist, and how Darius is convinced that the Mystery Man is his jailbird granddad, it all keeps swirling around in my head.

What does it all mean? And what am I doing, hanging with a totally whacked brainiac like Darius Drake? Okay, maybe it isn't his fault that he's weird, what with his parents dying and him being raised in an orphanage and all that. But that doesn't mean I should be part of it. Not with a human bulldozer like Scar Man involved, even if the big man is acting sort of friendly at the moment.

Must be I finally nodded off because the next thing I

know Mom is standing in my bedroom doorway, calling my name.

"Arthur, I hate to wake you on a Saturday morning, but you have a guest."

"Huh? Who?"

"Come down and find out. I'll make breakfast. Pancakes?"

Pancakes are always a yes. Are you kidding? But not even pancakes make me want to go downstairs and face the music, because I'm pretty sure who the guest must be. I mean, who else?

The red menace. The freckled maniac.

What finally gets me downstairs isn't the pancakes. It's the smell of bacon. Try as I might I can't resist bacon, even if it means facing Darius Drake before I've had my orange juice.

Except it's not him.

"Deirdre?"

"Good morning, Arthur," she says brightly.

"Huh," I say. "Hi."

I can't think of the last time Deirdre came to our house. The way it works, according to the divorce agreement, is I spend one night a week with my father at Deirdre's house, but she never spends time at mine. Not because my mom blames her for the divorce—Mom is way too fair to blame a child for something a parent did—but because, like I said, we come from different planets.

No tennis outfit for Deirdre today. But very girly. Skinny white jeans and a skinny pink top and her sunshine-colored hair neatly gathered into a ponytail that somehow says she's all business.

"Guess who came to see me?" she says, keeping her voice low. "Your friend Darius. The poor kid was really upset. He looked up your father's new address and tracked me down."

"Oh yeah?"

"When I mentioned to you that he officially died in the accident that killed his parents? That he was revived at the scene? I assumed he knew."

"He was too little to remember what happened."

"I get that now," she says, looking very serious. "Nobody ever told him the details, so it came as a shock. Apparently he's deeply embarrassed that something so tragic and personal is common knowledge. He wanted to know what else I'd heard, but really that's it: He died, and they brought him back. Isn't that enough?"

Mom clears her throat. She's standing there with a plate of steaming pancakes and a look of concern. "I couldn't help overhearing. It's none of my business, but just because a patient doesn't have a detectable pulse, it doesn't mean they 'officially died.' Not if they're quickly revived. And that was certainly the case with the Drake boy. As I recall he responded quickly to CPR."

Deirdre looks excited. "You were there?"

Mom nods. "On shift at the ER when they were brought in. Nothing we could do for his parents. The survivor, poor little boy, was revived at the scene, so we kept him under observation for several days, until his grandfather arrived to claim him."

"Pop Pop," I say. "That's what he called his grandfather."

"So he does remember?"

"Not the accident part," I say.

"That's a blessing," Mom says, setting the plate on the table.

All three of us dig in. Pancakes, bacon, butter, real maple syrup, what's not to like? I have two helpings. Okay, three. Mom smiles. Deirdre smiles. It's almost like we're a family.

Which we sort of are, I guess.

When we're done, I start to clear away the plates and load the dishwasher like usual, but Mom insists that just this once she'll take care of everything.

Deirdre waits until Mom is in the kitchen before leaning forward and speaking in a firm whisper. "One other thing you should know. I told your friend about this guy who came to my school to give a talk on local history? One of his less boring stories was about a treasure hunt. The search for a missing necklace."

"The Dunbar diamonds?"

Deirdre nods happily. "Wouldn't it be cool if you and Darius found the missing treasure?"

CHAPTER THIRTEEN

What Sisyphus Shared

FIVE MINUTES AFTER Deirdre splits, the doorbell rings.

"Arthur, can you get that? I have to get ready for my shift."

"Sure, Mom."

No surprise this time. Darius, with his eyes bloodshot from lack of sleep, or maybe allergies, and his hair even wilder than usual, as if it wants to escape from living on his head.

He waves a book in my face.

"See?" he says. "It was there all along. Nothing hidden inside. The clue was the book itself."

I carefully shut the front door behind me and edge him out into the yard. The less my mom knows about this the better. "Dude, you need to go home and get some sleep."

"Ha! Sleep is overrated. As you probably know, I consulted with your sister yesterday. Remarkable female. She suggested a new line of inquiry that has already proved fruitful."

"Yeah. Sorry, but I have chores today." That's lame and only sort of true.

"Our mission supersedes anything as mundane as chores," he announces, holding the book higher. *Donald E. Dunbar: His Life, Legend, and Legacy.* Your sister mentioned the author's name—apparently he spoke at her school. He may have crucial information, and he lives barely a mile from here."

"In a safe neighborhood?"

"Safe enough."

"Then why do you need *me*?"

That startles him. As if he hasn't considered the question. "Are you daft, Bash Man? Help me solve the mystery of who I am and we'll share the glory of recovering the Dunbar diamonds."

"That might not exist," I remind him.

"But what if they do?"

Maybe there's a good answer to that, one that will keep me out of trouble, but I don't know it.

————

The local history guy who spoke at Deirdre's school? He lives in Riverview Heights, in one of the houses built for factory workers a hundred years ago. The factories are gone, but the community of tidy brick houses remains, and most of them have been fixed up and improved over the years, so they no longer look quite so identical. For instance Mr. Robertson has converted his one-car garage into an office overlooking a small garden, and that's where he meets us.

"Right. This is for a school project, I assume? Have a seat."

He waves from his elevated desk, set on a platform surrounded by file cabinets. Like a bunker bristling with books instead of guns. He's an old dude with feathery white hair and a neatly trimmed white beard and weak-looking eyes blinking behind thick lenses. "Something about the Heights, is it? Local history project?"

Darius clears his throat. "Not precisely, no."

"No? Must have misheard. What then? Speak now or forever hold your peace. I'm a very busy man. Ha! I am Sisyphus, pushing an avalanche of paper uphill. And gravity always wins."

What can you say to that except "Huh?"

"Sisyphus," the old man says, raising his skinny finger like an exclamation point. "Character from Greek mythology. Doomed to spend eternity pushing a boulder uphill each day, and each day when he finally gets it to the top, the boulder rolls all the way back down. That's me, trying to keep up with all my assignments. Articles, papers, books, research, lectures. Granted, most of the files are electronic, but still they must be written, they must be read, they must be edited."

"Winston Brooks," Darius finally says.

"Forger and felon," Robertson responds brightly. "Charming fellow. I knew him well."

"He's my grandfather."

The mouth hidden inside the beard opens with astonishment. "You're his grandson? Are you, now? Well, well. Seems like yesterday, and yet here you are, nearly grown. Amazing what time does when I'm not paying attention."

"We're trying to locate him," Darius says. "I have many questions."

"No doubt. No doubt. Last I heard he'd been released from prison and moved back into his little place on Rutgers Road. Been meaning to drop by. Haven't gotten around to it. Busy, busy, busy."

Darius says, "He was there until recently, when he got sick. Supposedly he's staying someplace else till he gets better. I'm guessing he's in a nursing home or a rehab facility."

The old man looks crestfallen. "I'm very sorry to hear that. Winston and I had our disagreements, but I've always wished him well."

"The thing is, I've contacted every nursing facility in a fifty-mile radius. None of them have Winston Brooks as a patient."

The old man thinks about it. "It's possible your grand-father is using an alias. Quite possible."

"Why would he do that?"

The old man looks from Darius to me, as if trying to decide if we're old enough to hear something disturbing. Finally he nods to himself and goes, "Because he made such a mess of things. Such a terrible mess."

CHAPTER FOURTEEN

Why Trust a Criminal?

MR. ROBERTSON TAKES the book from Darius, taps his finger on the tattered cover. "It all started with this. My Dunbar bio. The man for whom our fair city was eventually named. Unfortunately the book didn't sell as well as I'd hoped, but Winston—your grandfather—read it cover to cover. The book gave him the germ of the idea, and soon he was reading everything he could find on the mysterious factory owner. Especially if it concerned the missing necklace."

Darius snorts. "So it was always about the money?"

Robertson shakes his head, amused. "Are you familiar with the fictional Indiana Jones? An archaeologist obsessed with finding treasure? Winston Brooks was the real-life version. He convinced himself that the Dunbar diamonds still exist and if he searched in the right places he would surely find them. But I can assure you that for Winston it wasn't about the money. It was the hunt, the search, the *finding*. That's what motivated him. But of course he needed a lot of money to finance the hunt, and that's what got him into trouble."

"Jasper Jones?"

"The very one. Runs some kind of investment fund, made a fortune when he was quite young, and then retired to an estate he built on Castle Island. Anyhow, Jones got bitten by the treasure bug, and your grandfather persuaded him to invest money in the hunt for the diamonds. Quite a lot of money."

Darius says, "But why did my grandfather need to borrow money? Why couldn't he just search for the diamonds?"

"Ah," the old man says. "We get to the crux of the matter. Winston had his theories about where the necklace might have been hidden, and to do a legal search meant acquiring property rights. Put simply, if he wanted to own the treasure he needed to buy the land where he thought it had been buried. First he bought the house on Rutgers Road, searched it top to bottom, and when that didn't pan out, he went in another direction. Bought another house and tore it down and dug halfway to China. And found nothing but dirt. It all cost money."

"But they say he forged documents."

The old man sighs and pauses to wipe his glasses. "I'm afraid he did. Your grandfather subscribed to a particular theory—that the necklace had been buried with the body of Lucy Dare, Dunbar's fiancée, in a tomb secretly constructed somewhere on Donald Dunbar's estate. But as I said, he couldn't dig up the property unless he owned it. Jasper Jones was willing to invest, but only if Winston had tangible proof that the diamonds were really somewhere on the property in question. So your grandfather tampered with an existing document, making it look like a reference to Lucy's burial place."

"He forged it," Darius says, stone-faced. "So there's no mistake. He was guilty."

The old man nods. "Guilty of believing his own theories. Guilty of promising something he had no certainty of delivering. But yes, guilty of forging a document and using it to obtain quite a lot of money. Poor man, his world fell apart in a single week. On Monday he was arrested. On Tuesday he was released on bail. And three days later his daughter—well, your parents—were killed."

I cringe at the phrase, but Darius doesn't react. Like when it comes to being an orphan, nothing can touch him. Not even when Mr. Robertson goes on to describe his parents.

"I knew them both," the old man says, voice softening. "Ellie and David. Ellie was taking care of her little boy—you—full-time while David finished graduate school. American literature, I believe. And when they weren't working or studying they were singing at various venues around town. Traditional folk music. Lovely voices, perfectly matched. That's how I knew them, originally. What a shame. What a loss."

Darius shakes his head almost furiously, as if to dislodge Robertson's kindly description of his parents. As if he finds sentiment distracting.

"Yes, fine, thank you," he says. "But what about this rich investor? Jasper Jones? What did he do?"

The old man gets up from his elevated desk and goes to the window, gazing out at his little garden. "He was upset about being deceived, but it was more than that. He was convinced your grandfather had found the diamonds and was concealing their location. Cheating him of the treasure itself."

"But you don't think so."

Mr. Robertson turns from the window, his watery eyes gleaming. "No, I do not."

"Why?" Darius asks. "Why trust a criminal?"

The old man considers the question. "Because I never thought of him that way. Despite the forged document and his money problems, Winston was in every other way an honest man. He sincerely believed he knew where Lucy Dare was buried. And if he'd recovered the diamonds, one thing is certain: He'd have announced it to the world. He would have alerted the media and held Dunbar's famous necklace up to the light. That's who he was."

"So he lied and he cheated, but he did not steal."

The old man stiffens, as if personally insulted. "You have cause to be angry, young man. More than most. But I know something that apparently you do not."

"Yeah?" Darius says, very sarcastic.

"Your grandfather loved you. You may not remember, because you were so young, but he took care of you for as long as he could. Until the last possible minute. Until the authorities removed you from his home and sent him off to prison."

CHAPTER FIFTEEN

He Went Wicked Gaga

TO BE HONEST I was never much interested in old stuff, or things that took place long before I was born. What's the point? It already happened. It's gone, dead, turned to dust. But I must admit, there was some pretty cool stuff in Mr. Robertson's book.

For instance, the part about tomb raiders trying to dig up the body of Lucy Dare, Donald Dunbar's fiancée, who died of influenza. Dunbar has mostly been forgotten, except for old history dudes like Mr. Robertson, but at one time he was really famous. Famous enough to get a city named after his famous factory. A celebrity, although they didn't call them that at the time. When he was seventeen years old, Dunbar invented a machine that stitched shoes together without the stitches showing. I don't know why that's important, but it made him a fortune, and by the time he was twenty years old, he had built Dunbar Mills, which, according to Mr. Robertson, was the largest fine-leather shoe factory in the world, and it employed more than half the people in our little city. High-fashion shoes and ladies' boots. Expensive stuff. And it made Dunbar very, very rich. In the early days he was seen at all the best places, hanging out with other rich and famous types. Despite numerous opportunities—he was basically the hot bachelor of his day—he never married. Never wanted to, apparently, until he met nineteen-year-old Lucy Dare in 1918, when the First World War was raging in Europe. Or, as Mr. Robertson called it, "the end-of-the-world war" because of all the deadly weapons unleashed by human technology: tanks, flamethrowers, machine guns, bombs dropped from airplanes, poison gas.

What blew my mind wasn't the war stuff—I'd read about that before, and it's sort of interesting in an awful way—but I was shocked to hear about Lucy Dare. She was an orphan. And you'll never guess where she grew up. The Stonehill Home for Children! Yes! Just like Darius. And like Darius she was thought to be the smartest of the children raised there, and the one with the most potential "to rise in the world, based on her intellect and character." Mr. Dunbar met Lucy Dare when she organized hospital volunteers to help care for the returning soldiers, and he fell for her big-time. The kids in my school would say he went wicked gaga. The newspapers reported that the "millionaire mill owner had finally met his match." He was quoted as saying, "Miss Dare is the most extraordinary person I've ever met. She has opened my heart for the first time. It was as if I was blind, and now, through her remarkable eyes, I see all the goodness in the world. Truly, I am smitten."

Smitten being the 1918 version of *wicked gaga*, right? Mr. Robertson provided lots of details from the society pages—the TMZ of the day—but the short version is that before leaving for England on a business trip, Donald Dunbar proposed to Lucy Dare and she accepted. He sailed on the *Aquitania*, a superfast ship, and sent her telegrams every hour on the hour, "exulting in her beauty, her intelligence, her grace, her goodness." (Had to look *exulting* up. Means "celebrating.") Once in England, the lovesick Dunbar (more like love-stupid if you ask me) did a quick tour of the factories that had used his inventions to manufacture boots and clothing for the war effort, and then stopped briefly in London before departing for home.

London is where Dunbar purchased the famous diamond necklace, which at the time was appraised for a million dollars, which is like fifteen million now, according to Mr. Robertson. The store where he bought it was in a place called Hatton Garden, the jewelry district, which also happens to be where the machine gun was invented and first manufactured. Interesting factoid, right? Anyhow, it was a fabulous necklace, loaded with diamonds and sapphires. Sky-blue sapphires to match her eyes, he was quoted as saying.

I know. Sappy stuff. And that's when it turns tragic, because between the time Dunbar left England with the necklace and returned home—a total of five days—Lucy Dare went and died. She had been directing volunteers at the hospital, where many of the soldiers were returning with a mysterious and deadly illness. It was the start of the great influenza pandemic that would kill as many as forty million people worldwide. At least half a million of those were right here in the United States, and Lucy Dare was one of the early victims.

Dunbar was devastated. He withdrew from public view and became a recluse, rarely leaving the grounds of his estate. His mills and factories gradually went under, and most were eventually torn down and sold for the bricks. Years went by. People sort of forgot about the Dunbar diamonds, until he died thirty years later, and the fabulous necklace was not found among his belongings. There was no record of it ever having been sold, so where was it?

That's when the speculation and rumors really got going. A story circulated that the necklace had been buried with Lucy Dare, as a token of his eternal love, and a few years after Dunbar croaked, her supposed grave was dug up, and guess what? No coffin! Either her coffin had been whisked away before it was buried, or Dunbar, fearful of grave robbers, had her buried at some secret location. So they decided to dig up Dunbar's grave, just to be sure he was really there, and guess what? Bingo! Also no coffin!

That's when the search for the Dunbar diamonds became a search for the real graves of Lucy Dare and Donald Dunbar. Treasure hunters came from all over, with all sorts of maps and theories, and according to Mr. Robertson, they dug more holes in local cemeteries than a scurry of rabid chipmunks. (That's what a group of chipmunks is called, a scurry. Who knew?)

Anyhow, nobody ever found the grave or the missing diamonds, and the whole thing gradually faded away until Darius's grandfather came along with a new theory about the location, and he revived the old treasure hunt for just long enough to forge a document, engage in financial fraud, and go to jail.

That's my book report, Darius. Take it or leave it, but either way, Bash Man is on the case, with or without candy bars.

(I hate that name but it sort of works, right?)

CHAPTER SIXTEEN

An Interesting Factoid

I KNOW WHAT you're thinking: This fatso dude is an idiot. A double-scoop dipstick, risking his life for a Snickers bar. Because anybody with half a brain can see that looking after a brainiac freak like Darius Drake is bound to get dangerous, sooner or later.

In this case, sooner.

Monday after school we go over to the library and check out the old newspaper files that nobody has bothered to put online, to see if we can find out anything else about Darius's grandfather Winston Brooks. Maybe identify an associate or friend who might know where the old treasure hunter is now. What nursing home or whatever.

Darius wants to call it "Operation Mystery Man."

"It helps to name a thing," he explains. "Gives it focus."

"How about 'Finding Pop Pop'?" I suggest.

Darius frowns. "Hey. I'm the brains, you're the brawn, remember?"

"Oh yeah? For your information I have a brain. And Operation Mystery Man is lame. In my humble opinion Finding Pop Pop sounds better."

"In your humble opinion."

"In my humble opinion."

Darius sighs and shakes his head. "It has a brain *and* an opinion. Who knew? Okay, you win; Finding Pop Pop it is."

———

To be honest, some of the stuff could have been researched from school, using online databases, but Darius wants to avoid the prying eyes of teachers. Even if it means messing up our own eyeballs by staring at microfilm files in the oldest part of the library. In case you've never had the pleasure, microfilm is old-style film on a spool—actual photos of each page of the printed-on-paper newspaper—that runs through this ancient projector screen. Sometimes the film is blurred or hard to read, hence the aching-eyeball problem.

"What year was your grandfather arrested?"

"The year my parents died. So what we're looking for must have happened in the months before that. Let's say the window is six months prior. Start there and go forward.

I'll start at the end and work back. We'll meet in the middle."

Less than an hour later, I come upon a front-page story about strange events that had occurred in Dunbar Acres, not far from my mom's house.

TREASURE HUNTER WINSTON BROOKS REFUSES TO be discouraged by failure, but the fate of the missing Dunbar diamonds is, for the moment, out of his grasp. Working from information provided by Mr. Brooks, his investment partners purchased a relatively new home located on the Lucy Dare cul-de-sac, in the Dunbar Acres subdivision. The cul-de-sac was named for the legendary recipient of the famed diamond necklace. According to Brooks, the diamonds should have been buried somewhere on the property. The entire fifty-acre subdivision was once the site of the Dunbar estate, which was razed in the 1970s. Mr. Brooks subscribes to the theory that famed inventor and factory magnate Donald Dunbar constructed a memorial tomb for the remains of his beloved, Lucy Dare, somewhere on the estate, and that the new home, a four-bedroom colonial, marked the secret location. But despite destruction of the house, deep excavation by heavy equipment, and further exploration with ground-penetrating radar devices, no sign of a grave or tomb was unearthed.

The project was halted by investors, who have lost faith in Mr. Brooks's theories about where the diamonds might be located.

"This was a bad day," Brooks admitted, but he vowed to continue his hunt for the treasure, with or without the backing of investors. "The diamonds are out there," he said. "This location has been eliminated, but there are other, even more promising leads."

Asked to elaborate, he declined to do so.

Listening to me read the article out loud, Darius shakes his head in disbelief. "They tore down a perfectly good house?"

"That's what it sounds like, yeah."

"No wonder his investors were ripped. What a waste."

"Yeah, but if they found the diamonds, he'd have been a hero."

"Except they didn't, and the whole project was based on a document he forged. Financial fraud is the same as stealing. He deserved to go to prison."

"That's harsh."

Darius shrugs, as if he couldn't care less. "An interesting fact, but it doesn't get us any closer to locating Mystery Man."

"You mean Pop Pop," I remind him.

"Whatever."

If I didn't know better, I might think Darius didn't want to find his grandfather at all.

CHAPTER SEVENTEEN

Finding Pop Pop

WE'RE LEAVING THE library and heading into town, thinking hot dogs and milk shakes, when an older-model Chevy Suburban pulls over, blocking our way. The tinted window rolls down, revealing the man with the melted face.

"Get in," says Scar Man, his massive hands on the steering wheel.

"To what purpose?" Darius edges away.

The big man snorts. "To the purpose I don't pound you into the ground like a tent peg, you little punk."

"Run," I suggest.

Scar Man rolls his eyes. "Yeah, go on, run. I ain't chasing you, not today. But let it be known the old man wants to see you. I'm doin' him a favor carrying you is all."

"You know where my grandfather is staying?"

"This is your last chance. See him or don't, no matter to me."

....

——

Yes, I know. It's the wrong thing to do, getting in that Suburban, but we do it anyway. It's not like Scar Man is some random serial killer. There's nothing random about him. And it's not like we're taking a ride with a stranger, because we know who he is. Which I guess means I can scrawl his name in my own blood, leaving a clue for the cops if things go south.

Bottom line, Darius wants to see his grandfather, and if that means trusting his life to the man with the melted face, he's willing to risk it. So we get in the back as instructed. Fasten our seat belts as instructed—turns out the big man is a fanatic for road safety.

Darius says, "How is he?"

Scar Man shrugs. "He been better. But it seem like the old dude ain't going to kick the bucket anytime soon."

"Huh," says Darius, who looks like he's doing calculations in his head. Like he can plug new information into some kind of formula, arrive at a conclusion. "How come you're helping him?"

Scar Man eyes us in the rearview mirror. Eyes like shiny black pebbles, and about as friendly. "That my business, boy."

"He's paying you to look after the house, right? Like protection money?"

The big man snorts. I never heard a bull snort, but it must be similar. "Not everything about money," he grumbles. "Most, but not all."

"So you and my grandfather are friends?"

"We acquainted. From prison, okay?"

"So you're doing this for free?" Darius says. "On a purely statistical basis, factoring in your reputation, I would judge the odds of that to be approaching zero."

"Huh? What you say?"

"You doing something for free. I highly doubt it."

The big man snaps his teeth like a pit bull eager to bite something, or somebody. "Time to shut up," he snarls.

The rest of the drive takes place in silence.

CHAPTER EIGHTEEN

Who Man Who

ACCORDING TO SCAR MAN, Winston Brooks checked into the Winter Pine Rehabilitation Facility under an assumed name, Howard Carter. The rehab facility isn't the run-down nursing home I'd been expecting, but an expanse of modern, single-story buildings linked like wheel spokes around a central treatment area. We find Mr. Howard Carter, aka Winston Brooks, in one of the residential spokes, in a nice room with a view of an artificial duck pond.

Just to be clear, the pond is artificial, but the ducks are real, quacking enthusiastically as they sport around the shallow pond.

Darius Drake's grandfather is a surprise, too. I'd been expecting a frail, sick old man. In my mind he would look something like Mr. Burns on *The Simpsons*, bald and bent over a cane. Instead, Winston Brooks has a head of thick, silver-streaked hair, worn in a neat, rubber-banded ponytail that ends between his shoulder blades. There are lines on his face, sure, but other than a bandaged leg, he looks fit and athletic. Not young, but not really *old* old. And strong for sure, like maybe he had lifted weights.

Oh yeah. Prison.

As for Darius, he doesn't know what to do. Whether he should shake hands—the man he once called Pop Pop has offered—or slap his grandfather's face for abandoning him to an orphanage and not coming to reclaim him as soon as he got out of prison.

I'd sort of been hoping they would hug it out, but there's no chance of that. Darius ignores the hand and keeps his distance. Mr. Brooks remains seated in a tall-backed chair, as if unsure what to do next. His left foot and leg, bandaged to the knee, are supported by an ottoman. There are crutches nearby. You can tell the leg still hurts him, even though he's trying not to show it.

"Long time no see," he says uneasily. Then he inhales deeply, as if savoring air that had touched his grandson.

"So. Who is Howard Carter?" Darius asks, folding his arms across his skinny chest as he stares straight ahead. Revealing no emotion. Cold as stone.

"Archaeologist," his grandfather says. "Discovered

King Tut's tomb in 1922. I needed to check in under an assumed name, and that seemed as good as any."

"Who are you hiding from?" Darius asks. "Me, by any chance?"

His grandfather looks startled. "Good Lord, no! Never that."

"Then why use a fake name?"

He shrugs, as if ashamed of himself. "Hiding from my past, you might say."

"So you did it. You were really guilty?"

Without hesitation, Mr. Brooks nods. "Oh yes. Guilty as sin. Guilty of forging a document and using it for financial gain. Guilty of cheating on my taxes. Guilty of arrogance. Guilty of self-delusion. Guilty of thinking that the ends would justify the means. Guilty of believing that if I managed to locate the Dunbar diamonds, nobody would care if the document that helped find them was a fake. That's what I told myself."

Darius stands there with his lips pursed, not responding for the moment. For some reason his reddish hair looks brighter than ever, as if maybe his brain is on fire, just beneath the roots.

"And who are you?" his grandfather says, turning his attention to me.

"I'm, ah, Arthur. Arthur Bash."

"My associate," Darius interjects.

"Associate? Vincent mentioned that you had been accompanied by a large, um, imposing-looking friend."

I wasn't sure what he meant by imposing-looking, but it was better than being described as a fat boy, that's for sure.

"When did you get out of jail?" Darius asks.

"Prison, not jail. About five months ago."

"And then you—what?—sent me a bloodstained letter?"

Winston Brooks looks startled. "What bloodstained letter?"

"The letter that said 'Who killed Darius Drake?' with a return address of 123 Rutgers Road."

Mr. Brooks looks like all the blood has drained from his face. "This is worse than I thought. Much worse. There's only one man who could have done such a thing."

"Scar Man?" Darius asks.

"Do they still call him that? How cruel. No, no, never him. He has a fearsome appearance, but I assure you that Vincent Meeks is a man of honor."

Darius snorts. "Honor among thieves?"

His grandfather winces. "Unlike me, Vinnie was never a thief. He was serving time for assault. A fight with some lowlife who had been taunting him. He was appealing the conviction on grounds of self-defense, and I helped him with some of the legal research. I got to know the man and his history—the disfigurement is from a childhood accident—and we became friends. He had been trying to persuade me to make contact and make amends, but I wasn't ready to face you, to be honest. Afraid you wouldn't remember me, and if you did, you'd hate me."

"I doubt you're worth hating," Darius says dismissively.

"My boy, I would do anything to change the past. But I can't. Please believe that."

"I'm not your boy. If it wasn't Scar Man, then who? You said there was only one man capable of such a thing."

His grandfather looks very distressed. "If I tell you, it will only make it worse."

"I'll find out," Darius says resolutely. "With your help or without it."

Mr. Brooks shakes his head. Clearly he doesn't want to say.

"What happened to your leg?" I ask, trying to break the tension. "My mom is a nurse."

He shrugs. "Blood clots formed in my lower leg. They call it deep vein thrombosis. Anyhow, a clot broke free and went up into my lungs. Almost killed me. The lung thing they fixed, then I almost lost my leg—no blood circulating."

"But you're okay now?" I ask.

"More or less," he says vaguely. "Another operation or two and I should be good to go."

Darius doesn't appear to be interested in his grandfather's medical history. Or his grandfather, for that matter. Which is weird because our whole mission was to locate the guy. Now we find him, and Darius is like—what?—too bored to care? Or maybe too angry about the bad stuff that happened when he was little?

Whatever, the situation is about as comfortable as having your underwear dusted with powdered fiberglass. And yes, that happened to me the only time I went to summer camp.

"If you're not going to tell me who sent the note, why did you send for me?" Darius asks, in a tone that says he couldn't care less.

"To beg you to stop looking for the Dunbar diamonds."

"We're still in the research stage."

"You need to drop it. You need to let it go."

"No chance," Darius says, folding his skinny, freckled arms across his chest.

"I'm begging you."

"Why should I listen to you?" Darius asks.

"Because your life may be at stake. I can't believe it, after all these years. I thought he'd moved on to other things. I thought he was done with me. That's the real reason I didn't contact you, because I didn't want to attract his attention. But it seems too late for that now."

"Who are you talking about?"

Winston Brooks's complexion has gone from pale to sick. The words seem to stick in his mouth. "Jasper Jones," he says, enunciating carefully. "The man who killed my darling daughter and her husband, and almost killed you."

CHAPTER NINETEEN

Happy Father's Day

DARIUS APPEARS TO be stunned. "My parents were killed in a car crash," he says. "Not murdered."

His grandfather nods. "Yes. But they were driving *my* car. Your dad's van was broken down, so I loaned them mine." He buries his face in his hands, and then shudders, as if awakening from a nightmare. "I've never been able to prove it, but I have reason to believe someone ran them off the road, thinking it was me. Or to punish me in the worst way possible."

"Jasper Jones. The man you cheated."

The old treasure hunter sighs. "Believe the worst of me if you must. But I'm begging you, stay away from the Dunbar diamonds."

"Because you already know where the diamonds are hidden?"

He shakes his head firmly. "No, no. If I did, I'd hand them over to Jasper and be done with it."

Darius jams his hands in his pockets and walks in a tight circle, like a small, angry planet orbiting a sun it doesn't trust. "Let me see if I can follow the logic," he says. "I'm close to solving the puzzle that ruined your life, and you beg me to stop. How does that make sense? And why should I believe anything you say?"

Silence. If only I could melt into the floor, or turn invisible, or maybe go deaf. Because hearing them talk around each other is like getting poked with a sharp stick. It hurts in familiar places, even though I'm not an orphan like Darius, or a felon like Winston Brooks, aka the Mystery Man, aka Pop Pop.

"I really messed this up," he says, forlorn. "Seven and a half years inside, all I thought about was making it right. I had this fantasy we could continue where we left off. You were my little buddy, Darry, in that year after the accident, before I got sentenced. It was just you and me, both of us grieving but making the best of it. And then they took you away and put me away. Sent to our own prisons, you might say."

Darius sneers dismissively. "Stonehill is no prison! As a place to live goes, it is entirely satisfactory. I wouldn't want to be anywhere else."

His grandfather brightens. "Seriously? I'm glad to hear

it. I thought you'd be in good hands until they found you a foster home. You were such an angry little boy, they warned me that you might be difficult to place, but I never expected you'd grow up there."

"I have no interest in a foster family," Darius says airily. "I'm better off alone."

His grandfather's eyes are wet. He suddenly appears to be very tired. "Nobody is better off alone," he says quietly.

"I'm the exception," Darius snaps. "Enough of this sentimental junk! Tell me why I should believe that the man you cheated is a threat to me."

His grandfather sits up a little straighter, clears his throat. "Because he said so. He vowed to ruin my life, and that included my family. It wasn't a matter of paying back the money he invested. He wanted the diamonds, and nothing else would do. Jasper puts on a good show, everybody thinks he's a great guy, very generous and involved in the community, but you want to know what kind of man he really is? The day after your parents were killed, he came to the hospital. You were still undergoing tests. Crying out for your mommy and daddy. It was heartbreaking. Awful, awful, awful. So Jasper saunters in, and he takes me by the arm, and he whispers in my ear. 'This is only the beginning,' he says. Not *Sorry for your loss*. Or *How is the boy?* 'This is only the beginning.' And it was. He made sure I was prosecuted to the full extent of the law. No mercy, no chance to pay back the money. And his lawyers made sure there was no real investigation of the accident."

"What was there to investigate? What proof did you have that Jasper Jones was involved?"

"There were parallel skid marks at the crash site that indicated another vehicle might have run them off the road. The state police investigated, but Jasper brought in expert witnesses who discounted the tire marks, and I had no money to hire expert witnesses of my own. By that time I was out on bail, awaiting trial, and my whole focus was taking care of a little boy who had been terribly traumatized."

"Huh. Is that supposed to make me feel guilty?"

"No! Absolutely not. I'm just stating the facts. I can't prove it, but I know in my heart that Jasper had something to do with the crash. He's convinced that I'm holding out on him, that I have the Dunbar diamonds, and he won't stop tormenting me until he has them in his possession. No matter what it takes, or who he has to harm. He's more obsessed with those diamonds than I ever was."

Darius strides over, dry-eyed and arrogant. "I ask again, what proof do you have? Not whispered threats from years ago, but something that proves he's currently a threat to you, or to me, or to anyone?"

His grandfather shakes his head, like he's having trouble accepting that Darius is so cold and disdainful. "Not proof, exactly. But this was sent to me on Father's Day."

He fiddles with the bandage covering his leg and extracts what looks like an ordinary Father's Day card. Creased and wrinkled but still legible.

On the outside, a sappy photograph of a father and young daughter playing catch, and the words *The Best Day of My Life.*

On the inside, cutout words had been pasted into a message that couldn't be more clear.

GIVE ME WHAT I WANT, OR
THE BOY WILL JOIN HIS MOTHER.

HAPPY FATHER'S DAY.

CHAPTER TWENTY

Infinitely Worse

WE HEAD BACK to Stonehill in the old Suburban. The first mile or two unfurls in uncomfortable silence, until Scar Man clears his throat and says, "That old man loves you, boy. You his main topic of conversation, from the first day we cross paths. His brilliant grandson, and how bad he felt for failing you. The man ain't perfect—no man is—but he got your best interest in his heart."

"Oh yeah?" Darius says, staring out the tinted window, watching the world glide by.

The big man shakes his head. "Maybe you got a right to be angry. But if you're as smart as he say, you'll stay far away from Jasper Jones. From what your grandpop say, that man is pure evil."

"I'll think about it," Darius says.

The Suburban leaves us near the front steps of the library and takes off in a spray of driveway gravel.

"I don't think Scar Man likes us very much," I say, and try to fake a clever chuckle, *heh-heh-heh*. Probably sounds like I'm puking pebbles.

"His opinion is of no consequence," Darius says dismissively. "We have a new direction, and a new goal."

I'm afraid to ask, but for once that doesn't stop me.

"We're going to locate Jasper Jones and observe him," Darius explains, "with the goal of determining if my grandfather is correct in his assessment, or if he's still lying."

I'm confused. "But why would he lie to you?"

Darius snorts. "Obviously he still wants the Dunbar diamonds. And he wants me to find them."

"Huh? How do you figure that?"

"Because he told me not to look for them."

"I don't get it."

"My grandfather took care of me for a year—right?— after the accident? Just him and me? So he knows from experience that telling me not to do something virtually guarantees that I will do it."

"Really? That just sounds stupid."

"Not stupid," he says patiently. "Perfectly logical."

"Logical to check out a guy who maybe killed your parents?"

He smiles. "I knew you'd understand. Now, please, let's concentrate on finding the elusive Mr. Jones."

———

Turns out that Jasper Jones's location isn't exactly a state secret. When I mention his name to Deirdre she sounds impressed. "How do you know Jasper? He's a really cool guy."

"I don't know him, but he was involved with the search for the Dunbar diamonds."

"For real?"

"Not now," I say. "Back in the day."

"So what do you want with him?"

"He's our designated surveillance subject."

Deirdre laughs. "That's obviously Darius, not you."

"Officially known as the DSS."

"Really? Actually that's sort of cool, I think. Unless it gets you into trouble."

"Strictly an observational mission."

This time Deirdre can't help it. She rolls her eyes. "Well, the good news is this: He won't be hard to find. He lives on the biggest estate on Castle Island. If he's not there, he'll be at the Castle Island Tennis Club. He owns the place."

———

Couple of things you should know about Castle Island. It's not really an island—connecting land was filled in years ago—and there's no castle. What it does have is a bunch of really rich people, millionaires and even a few billionaires.

Castle Island isn't a gated community, exactly, because the scenic roadway that winds through it is a state road, and therefore open to the public. But most of the homeowners have electronic gates and security, including hedges so high you can't see the houses and the guesthouses and the boathouses and the servants' quarters.

I'm kidding about servants' quarters. These days the help are bussed in from the poorer parts of the city, or from Home Depot parking lots where they're looking for a day's work. Or anyhow that's what Deirdre says, and she ought to know, from her experience visiting the homes of her posse from the tennis club.

"I don't have a posse," she says, scornful of the notion. "Please."

"Sorry."

"You want to do this thing?" she asks, expertly changing the subject. "Come on. No time like the present."

———

The tennis club is about three miles from town. I suppose we could have walked it, but it just so happens that Deirdre has a tennis lesson on Saturday afternoon, so it makes sense if we tag along as her guests.

And we travel by hired car, no less. I could get used to this. It feels really smooth having a stepsister with her own Uber account. And for once Darius keeps his mouth shut.

I've never seen him back down from anyone, but with Deirdre in close proximity he gets real quiet.

The Uber car drops us off at the gate. Of course the tennis club has a security gate. Have you been paying attention? Castle Island, private club?

Long story short, Deirdre buzzes us through on her card and walks us into the clubhouse, which, no surprise, overlooks the tennis courts.

"We have a family membership," she says. "Use my name, order a lemonade or whatever. I'll be on court seven, getting my butt kicked by the pro. The guy you want to see, Jasper Jones? Like I said, he's a really cool guy."

"What's so cool about him?" Darius asks, sounding a teeny bit jealous.

"See for yourself. That's him at the clubhouse café. Third table from the left. The one with the rescue dog."

It would have been hard to miss him, even without the cute yellow Labrador. The dude looks like a movie star. One of those actors who are so cool and fun that being older than your parents doesn't matter. In particular an actor who played a treasure-hunting pirate, hungry for jewels, and who dealt with the dead on a regular basis.

Jack Sparrow himself. He's the spitting image of Johnny Depp.

CHAPTER TWENTY-ONE

The Lion in His Den

WE SIT AT this little table in the outdoor café overlooking the tennis courts, under a bright green umbrella, sipping fresh-squeezed lemonade and pretending not to stare at Jasper Jones. He's not Johnny Depp, of course, but he sure looks a lot like him, and maybe on purpose, if the length of his hair and his perfect tan and his hip sunglasses are any indication. Although, to be fair, he's not dressed like a pirate or anything. He's wearing some kind of silky, pastel-colored shirt that looks like it was made only for him, and pleated linen slacks with a perfect crease. Plus those snazzy sunglasses that are definitely not off-the-rack.

My first thought is, I wouldn't mind trading places with Mr. Jones. Not only is he obviously rich, but he's also super casual and friendly. Everybody seems to know and like him. Bartenders, waitresses, club members, they all stop to chat and pet the dog, and bask in that movie-star smile.

Yes, it would be cool to be Jasper Jones.

"What do you think?" Darius asks in a low voice.

"About what?"

"This. Being flies on the wall."

"Are you sure this is the right guy? Your grandfather made it sound like he's really dangerous."

Darius shakes his head. "He doesn't look dangerous. Unless wearing expensive clothes is dangerous."

"Dude," I whisper urgently, "I totally agree. But what if your grandfather is right? What if he's the one who sent you the bloody note? And that awful card to your grandfather?"

"That's what we're here to find out."

"What are you going to do? Ask him if he's an evil villain in disguise?"

"Maybe I will," he says.

But Jasper Jones beats us to it. Before we have a chance to finish our lemonades, he gets up from his table, adjusts his fabulous shades, and saunters directly over to our little table. The yellow Lab timidly follows, keeping up with the leash.

"I'm Jasper Jones," he announces, reaching out his hand. "Welcome to the club. This is Blondi. She's a rescue dog, but we've been going to therapy dog classes for the last few months and now she likes to be petted."

The dog looks at us warily, as if sizing us up, and then

abruptly settles her head on my knee. I pet her, very gently, and she makes a sound of contentment deep in her throat.

As usual I'm doing my best to avoid eye contact with grown-ups, but Darius meets his gaze defiantly. This gangly kid with thick glasses and a spewing volcano of bright red hair. I shouldn't say that my friend looks goofy and out of place in the exclusive tennis club, but he sort of does. And he doesn't care. Not one bit.

"Hello, Mr. Jones," Darius says, shaking hands. "I'm Darius Drake. This is my associate, Arthur Bash."

Mr. Jones smiles and says, "I see Blondi has taken a shine to you, Arthur. She came into my shelter a year ago, underweight and scared of her own shadow. Lately she's come out of her shell and is learning to make new friends."

"You run a rescue shelter?" Darius asks. "I thought you were some kind of big-shot banker."

Jones looks amused. "Not a banker, exactly. Wealth management. My day job is helping people find ways to invest their money, but my passion is animals. I don't run the shelter, I just help fund it."

The Lab slips her head off my knee and returns to Jones, leaning against his leg as if she'd like to blend right into him. "Do you mind if I join you?" he asks.

"It's your club," Darius says, sounding flippant.

Mr. Jones pulls up a chair, settles the dog at his feet. "To be honest, Darius, I recognized you. You probably don't pay attention to such things, but I'm on the advisory board at Stonehill. Doubtful you'd remember, but we met many years ago, when you were a toddler."

Darius shrugs, neither confirming nor denying.

Jones smiles with his perfect, movie-star teeth. "If you'd like to play tennis or use the pool, I can get you some complimentary passes."

That sounds good to me, at least the pool part, but Darius shakes his head. "No. We're just here because Deirdre says this place has the best lemonade in town."

"Deirdre?" he says. "Oh yeah. Cute kid. Decent serve; has a solid backhand. Whatever the reason, I'm delighted you stopped by." He hesitates, fiddles with his sunglasses. "If you don't mind me asking, how's Winston doing? Your grandfather, Winston Brooks."

"What about him?" Darius says.

"I heard he was sick. Something about blood clots? Where's he being treated? I'd like to send him a get-well card."

"Maybe you already did," Darius says.

Jones looks puzzled.

"A Father's Day card," Darius says. "Remember?"

"Why would I send Winston a Father's Day card?" Jones shakes his head and sighs. "Wait, let me guess. Some things never change. He wants you to believe I threatened him."

Darius crosses his skinny arms and looks Mr. Jones right in the eye. Or at least right in his sunglasses. "The card read, 'Give me what I want, or the boy will join his mother,' " he says.

Jones jerks back in the chair, as if repulsed by the idea. "Be assured I'd never send such a note! I have no reason to threaten you or anyone. What happened with your grandfather, that was long ago and best forgotten."

"But you haven't forgotten," Darius says defiantly.

"No," Jones admits. "I'm only human. Your grandfather defrauded me. My investors lost money. I lost money. So, no, I haven't forgotten."

"And you still want the money back. Or the necklace."

Jones sighs. "The money is gone and there's no getting it back. As to the so-called Dunbar diamonds, they're a figment of Winston's deluded imagination. The necklace is a mirage he's been chasing all his adult life, and it keeps vanishing because it's an illusion. Once upon a time he persuaded me to share in that illusion—hunting for a lost treasure, how exciting!—but I finally came to my senses. No more treasure hunts, no more crazy treasure hunters."

"You're saying my grandfather is crazy?"

Jones cocks his head sideways, thinking about it before replying. "Let me put it this way. There's a fine line between obsession and delusion, and Winston crossed that line years ago. Part of Winston's delusion involves blaming me for all his problems. He wants you to share the delusion, and that involves thinking the worst of me. So he did what he always does when his back is against the wall: He forged a document—a Father's Day card, you say?—and pointed you in my direction."

"We came on our own," Darius says.

Mr. Jones shakes his head sorrowfully. "You may think you did, but if the past is any indication, Winston has some sort of agenda in mind. His ideas can be very difficult to resist. Believe me, I know. What else did he tell you about me? What else does he want you to believe?"

"That you still want the Dunbar diamonds."

"As I said, your grandfather had me convinced, but the spell was broken long ago. I moved on to other opportunities."

Darius leans forward. "What if I know where they are? Would you be interested?"

Mr. Jones looks startled. He raises his sunglasses, and the resemblance to Johnny Depp fades a bit. Eyes a little too small. "Seriously? You're kidding me, right? Did your grandfather send you here to ask me that? Is that your mission?"

"My grandfather didn't send me. Quite the opposite."

Jones looks resigned, but resolute in his answer. "Let me be clear, young man. I no longer have any interest in those cursed diamonds. They've brought nothing but trouble into this world. Trouble for Winston Brooks, trouble for me. If by some miracle you manage to recover the Dunbar diamonds, do whatever you want with them."

Blondi makes a slight whimpering noise and nuzzles against his leg. Jones caresses her furry neck and the whimpering stops.

"One more question, Mr. Jones," Darius says. "Did you kill my parents?"

CHAPTER TWENTY-TWO

One Final Question

JASPER JONES LOOKS stunned. He takes a deep breath and sighs. "No, of course not. Absolutely not! Your parents died in a tragic road accident. But Winston refused to believe the facts. He put the blame on me."

Winston. Mystery Man. Pop Pop. Darius's grandfather has so many names it's hard to remember them all. That alone is suspicious, right?

Darius asks, "Why did he refuse to believe the facts?"

Jones considers the question. "I guess you're mature enough to know the true circumstances, and you certainly deserve to. The truth is, your parents came to see me the night they died. It was your mother's idea, begging mercy for her father. She wanted me to intervene somehow, to get the charges dropped. They were a very appealing young couple, by the way, and of course they had a cute toddler along—you—so it was very hard to refuse. But I'm afraid I had to do so. I wasn't the only one who was defrauded—all of my investors took a loss. It wasn't up to me to interfere with the course of justice."

"My grandfather says that you used your influence to make sure he got the maximum sentence."

Jones shakes his head sorrowfully. "That never happened. Not at all. Of course I had to look out for my own investors, but I'm not a vindictive man."

"Why should I believe you instead of him?"

"Well, for starters, because I'm not a criminal. I don't have a history of defrauding people. And upset as I was to be swindled out of so much money, I'd never do anything so cruel. It's just not me." He pauses to carefully clean his sunglasses, as if taking the time to gather his thoughts. "I've no idea what Winston Brooks truly believes or doesn't believe. Maybe he has convinced himself that I'm the cause of all his problems. Maybe he's so overcome by guilt that he can no longer see reality."

"Reality?"

Jones nods solemnly. "Guilt not just for his crime, but for all that flowed from it. If he hadn't defrauded his investors, your parents wouldn't have driven out on a rainy night to plead his case."

"So it was his fault my parents were killed?"

"Sadly, it was. I'm sorry, Darius, but your grandfather's obsession with the Dunbar diamonds led him to break the law. Maybe he didn't intend that others would be hurt as a consequence of his lies and deceptions, but they were. It must prey heavily on his mind. That would explain him being so . . . disturbed. He can't face the truth, so he blames me."

"But why would he believe that you could be a danger to me?"

Jones looks baffled. "I haven't the faintest idea. It's ridiculous, of course. As I say, I remember you as a toddler. Cute little guy. Your hair was red even then, as I recall. Why would I wish you harm?"

"What if I found the Dunbar diamonds? Would you wish me harm then?"

Mr. Jones is obviously starting to lose his patience, and his smile fades. "No, of course not. Why should I? Why, have you located the diamonds?"

"Not yet."

"Not yet. I see. You think you can succeed where a hundred grown men and women have failed? Well, who knows? You're supposed to be a very clever boy, maybe you can. But if you do, the real danger may lie with your grandfather. Not him personally—I mean some of the criminals he befriended in prison."

"Who do you mean?" Darius says, stirring uneasily.

"The big man from the Stompanado projects." Jones

touches the right side of his face. "The one they call Scar Man?"

"What about him?"

"Darius, please listen to me. Stay away from him. He's a violent felon. The kind of man who'd wait his chance to swoop in and steal the Dunbar diamonds for himself, if they even still exist."

Darius has the look he gets when he's thinking hard. Calculating. "That's a real possibility," he finally concludes. "But how do you know who my grandfather befriended in prison?"

Jasper Jones smiles. "I wish it were otherwise, but I'm afraid people will always associate me with that failed treasure hunt. The house that was destroyed, the holes dug, the money lost. My disastrous partnership with your grandfather was well-known. People tell me things. And a man as big and scary as Scar Man is hard to miss."

"So you haven't been keeping an eye on him yourself?"

"Why would I?" says Jones, looking puzzled.

"Because you believe my grandfather is holding out on you. That he found the diamonds but refused to give you your share."

Jones snorts. "Of all the things your grandfather did, all the lies he told, that's the biggest whopper of all."

Darius stares at Jasper Jones, his expression unreadable.

"True or false," he says, his voice flat. "The day after the accident that killed my parents, you went to see my grandfather in the hospital and said, quote, 'This is just the beginning.'"

Jones shrugs. "It's true that I went to the hospital to visit him. Of course I did, it was a terrible tragedy. But I never said anything remotely like that. No decent person would threaten a man at a time of such grief."

"Then why did he say you did?"

Jones looks helpless. "How could I possibly know what motivates him? But it's obvious your grandfather has convinced himself that I'm to blame for all his problems. Maybe he can't face up to the truth."

"And what is the truth?"

Jones clears his throat and says, "As I told you a moment ago, if your grandfather Winston Brooks hadn't broken the law, his daughter wouldn't have been out on a rainy night, pleading for mercy. Your parents would still be alive, Darius. *That's* the truth."

CHAPTER TWENTY-THREE

Back in the Stacks

GOOD THING WE have access to the Uber car, courtesy of Deirdre. No way can I walk three miles with my knees shaky like I haven't eaten. But the whole confrontation makes me so nervous I'm not even slightly hungry. Two kids demanding answers from a wealthy and powerful adult? Not my kind of thing at all.

We don't talk much during the ride back, me and Darius, but after the car drops us off at Stonehill he turns to me and asks, "What do you think? Is he right about Scar Man?"

"I don't know."

"It fits into my working theory, and it would explain why Scar Man always seems to be lurking around."

"So would friendship," I say.

"What?"

"Him and your grandfather being friends. That would explain it."

Darius looks puzzled, as if the concept of friendship eludes him. "Let's put that aside for the moment, and concentrate on the immediate situation. Scar Man, a violent felon, may pose a threat."

"Great," I say. "Wonderful."

"No, no. It could be useful. We know that under the right circumstances, Scar Man has an explosive temper. If Jasper Jones is right about him, maybe we can use that to our advantage."

"Really? Are you serious? You want to get him to go postal on us? What, so he can be arrested after we're dead?"

"Nothing so dramatic," Darius says. "Not quite."

————

Next morning we're heading back to the Registry of Deeds, in search of more information about the house at Rutgers Road. All part of the plan, Darius assures me, but he won't go further than that.

"One step at a time," he says.

"Yeah, but what if that one step is on a land mine?"

"Chill, okay? We're going to be fine."

"And how do you know that?" I ask, really wanting to know.

Darius sighs. "That should be obvious. Because I'm

significantly more intelligent than our quarry, whoever he may be. Scar Man, Jasper Jones. Or my own grandfather."

"You can't mean that," I say, shocked.

"Facts are facts," he says stubbornly. "And the fact is, my grandfather can be untrustworthy. He might be telling the truth; he might not."

"Dude, I know you're smart. Wicked smart. You're so smart your brain has a brain. But your grandfather is pretty smart, too, and he said we shouldn't look for the diamonds. What if he's right?"

Darius's eyes look even bigger than usual behind his thick lenses. Like a couple of blue planets staring at me from outer space. "Really? You have so little faith in my powers of deduction? Suck it up, Bash Man. You're braver than you think."

"Yeah? What makes you think so?"

"I just do. When the time comes—*if* the times comes—there's a ninety-seven percent probability that you'll do the brave thing. Now, let's get down to business, shall we? The facts convince me that the key to recovering the Dunbar diamonds is somehow connected to the house on Rutgers Road. That will be our line of inquiry, and our task is to gather all available intelligence. Starting with who owned the property before my grandfather purchased the place and put it in my name."

The search for information is easier the second time, which makes sense. We already know our way around the lower level of the Registry of Deeds, and what to expect as we search the index books, looking for a match.

"How very strange," Darius says, closing one of the giant, leather-bound books. "The earliest property tax entry for 123 Rutgers Road seems to be in 1934, but the house was built much earlier than that, near the turn of the twentieth century."

"How do you know that?"

He shrugs. "Lots of little indicators. The electrical wiring in the basement is of a type not used after about 1930. Much the same for the original plumbing connections. They date to much earlier."

"Wow," I say, shaking my head. "It's amazing you'd know junk like that. Did you get it from an online source?"

He chuckles. "From *This Old House* on TV."

With the index ledgers a dead end, we go back to the original land maps, and that's where I make my contribution. "Huh," I say. "Looks like Rutgers Road wasn't always Rutgers Road. See? In 1918 it was called Dunbar Mills Road."

Darius steadies his glasses and peers at the map. "Well done, Bash Man! And there it is, see? That little square must be the old house. Look how close it was to the original factory complex."

The old factory buildings are gone, of course, taken down to make way for the Stompanado housing projects. But once upon a time the high brick walls of one of the biggest factories in the world would have put that house in shadow for most of the day.

A shadow that still seems to be there, despite the factory being gone.

Darius rushes back to the deed ledgers, armed with the new—or rather the original—address, and soon he announces he's got it. "The original property owner is listed as James G. Rutgers, on a house lot deeded to him in 1905 by—get this—Dunbar Mills, Incorporated."

The air is pretty warm in the stacks, but a shiver goes down the back of my neck. "So they're all connected," I say. "James Rutgers, Donald Dunbar, Lucy Dare, and the missing diamonds."

"Agreed. But how?"

"I don't know. But whoever James Rutgers was, they renamed the road for him."

CHAPTER TWENTY-FOUR

The Witch
House Clue

WE FIND MR. ROBERTSON buried under a stack of paper. Okay, that's an exaggeration. He isn't completely buried. His white-bearded face pokes up from his desk, blinking blurry-eyed at us from between tall stacks of books and papers.

"Busy," he mutters, fingers flying over a keyboard. "Whoever you are, come back when I'm not on deadline."

"When will that be?"

"After I'm dead. Until then, write I must, as Yoda would say."

"It's a matter of life and death!"

He pauses and squints, bringing us into focus. "Isn't it always? Oh. I know you. Sherlock and Watson. No, wait, the Drake boy and his, what did you call him, *associate*? Good a word as any, I suppose. Hmmm, life and death, you said. Are you in immediate danger?"

"Quite plausibly," Darius says, approaching the fully loaded desk. "Although it's not clear who might be dangerous. But we did promise Jasper Jones that we'd find the Dunbar diamonds."

Mr. Robertson sighs and leans back, lacing his long fingers together as he thinks it over. "There it is," he says. "History repeats itself. Winston has passed you the torch."

"I did this on my own. My grandfather disapproves."

"Oh? Good for him. The diamonds have been missing for almost a hundred years. Scores of treasure hunters and tomb raiders have failed, including Winston Brooks. What makes you think you can find them?"

"By utilizing the process of inductive reasoning."

"Excuse me?"

"We'll look where they haven't," Darius explains. "And develop likely theories based on observation. What can you tell us about James Rutgers?"

Mr. Robertson smiles at the name. "Ah! I see where you may be going with this. Did you check my index? Yes, of course you did. That's why you're here."

The old historian is referring to the index in his biography of Donald Dunbar. *Rutgers, James, Millwright* had twenty-six entries. Whereas *Dare, Lucy* was mentioned only nineteen times.

"If you checked the index and read the entries, then you already know how important Mr. Rutgers is to the story of

Dunbar Mills. He and Donald Dunbar were lifelong friends. They were from the same neighborhood, attended the same elementary school, the same vocational school. Dunbar was the genius, thinking up new ways to manufacture shoes and boots and clothing, but it was James Rutgers who implemented his ideas. Rutgers built the actual machines. Which, as you know—assuming you've read my book—is what a millwright does. Nowadays the term is little known outside the trades, but in the world of factories and manufacturing, millwrights remain essential. Without them, nothing of importance gets built or made. A millwright is part engineer, part builder, part craftsman. James Rutgers was all those things, and a very clever man to boot. Pun intended! Shoe factory, boot, get it?"

Darius ignores the lame-o joke. "What can you tell us about his house?"

"Ah, the witch house," Mr. Robertson says. "That's what we called it when I was a boy. Because the peaked roof looks like a witch's hat. What do I know? Not much, I'm afraid. I know it was built on land that once belonged to the factory. James Rutgers ran the factory, so it made sense that he lived nearby. I haven't checked the land deeds, but I assume Dunbar gave it to him, or sold it to him."

"A gift," Darius says.

Mr. Robertson nods. "What we know is this: James Rutgers lived in that house until his death. Passed away only a year after Dunbar. End of an era, and a sad end at that. By then the factory was abandoned, all the great machinery sold for salvage and carted away. Rutgers was a bachelor, married to his job, with no heirs, and I believe the property was eventually forfeited to the city, for failure to pay taxes. And there it stood for decades. Nobody wanted the place, until Winston came along, and he got it for almost nothing. He was convinced the house contained some clue to the location of the diamonds, and that he would find it. As far as I know, he never did. But he was clever enough to deed it to you the day before he was arrested, otherwise it would have been seized to pay his debts."

Darius nods to himself, as if the story confirms his own conclusions. "My grandfather was pretty smart," Darius says. "If my theory is correct, he was heading in the right direction, but he failed to see the big picture."

"Did he now? How so?" Mr. Robertson says, looking over the tips of his steepled fingers.

"The clue is the house itself," Darius says.

CHAPTER TWENTY-FIVE

Knock Knock

SOME FAMOUS DUDE once said the only thing we have to fear is fear itself. I'm pretty sure he never saw Scar Man flexing his big tattoos.

"See this fist? You go against what Winston say, and risk your life, this fist gone pound you into the ground headfirst."

Darius lifts his freckled chin, as if welcoming a blow. "Wouldn't dream of it. Stand aside, please."

I'm not sure if *Tyrannosaurus rex* growled, but if so it must have sounded a lot like Scar Man as he shows us his fangs. Excuse me, his grillz. Or maybe he really has titanium teeth, I wouldn't put it past him. Whatever, he's not exactly happy to see us.

"I'm the lawful owner of this property," Darius says, showing him the key.

"Winston say you're after them diamonds and it gonna get you killed."

"Has my grandfather searched this house? Many times? From top to bottom?"

"You know he has."

"Ergo the treasure can't be here, ergo we won't be risking our lives."

"Ergo my butt! Don't you get it? Them diamonds is cursed. Got a power to ruin lives. Can't you see that, you snarky little punk?"

"Shall I summon an officer of the law? No? Then stand aside, please."

Incredibly enough, the big man does just that. Although not without a lot of grumbling. But what surprises me even more is what happens when we get inside the house and lock the door behind us.

Darius starts to tremble like a leaf.

"Dude, what's wrong?"

It takes him a while to form a reply. "Truth? That man really scares me."

"Are you serious? So that was an act, you standing up to him? Amazing! I never guessed."

Makes me wonder about in school, when bullies taunt him and it seems like he couldn't care less—is that an act, too?

It feels sort of good, knowing I'm not the only one pretending to be brave. But part of me wonders if Scar Man has the right idea. Maybe the diamonds really are cursed. Right from the beginning. The owner of Dunbar Mills buys the love of his life the fanciest, most expensive necklace in the world, and she dies within a few days. *Curse?* His famous factory ultimately failed. *Curse?* Winston Brooks searches for the lost diamonds and goes to prison. *Curse?* His daughter and her husband are killed in a crash. *Curse?* Darius grows up an orphan. *Curse?*

Darius must be reading my mind, because he says, "Don't even think about it. We'll solve this mystery if it kills us."

"That's what I'm afraid of."

"Well, don't be." Darius has recovered himself and looks grimly satisfied as he settles into one of the over-stuffed chairs. "For decades treasure hunters have gone after these diamonds with picks and shovels and backhoes and dynamite. We're going to locate them with brain-power, and without leaving this house."

"Right."

"Have a little faith, Bash Man," he says, tapping the side of his head. "We have the technology."

"Brainpower?"

He nods. "Sir Isaac Newton discovered the law of universal gravitation by a process of thought he called inductive reasoning. Unlike the more common deductive reasoning, the inductive process begins with observation and then proceeds toward theory. Newton observes an apple falling from a tree, thinks about what that might mean—why does it fall, what causes it to fall, how does this apply to the world, to the universe?—and uses that simple observation to calculate the law of gravity. Surely we can discover some missing jewels by using the same process."

"Okay, but you should know I don't have a clue what you're talking about."

"It's not that complicated," Darius says. "We gather the facts of the case, weigh them as to relevance and probability, and then draw conclusions."

"If you say so."

"This may take some time," he says. "And a considerable exertion of brainpower. Sustenance is definitely required."

He reaches into a pocket, produces two Snickers bars, and hands me one.

So maybe this inductive reasoning thing isn't so bad, not if it involves candy bars. My mouth is watering, and I'm about to chomp down on the first bite—mmm good, can't wait—when a fist pounds on the front door.

CHAPTER TWENTY-SIX

The Trouble with
the Future

DEIRDRE IS ON the front steps, smiling impishly. She's wearing a pink hoodie with the hood up and a baseball cap. "A treasure hunt? And you forgot to invite me? That's seriously rude!"

I pull her into the house and shut the door, heaving a sigh of relief. Then it dawns on me that if Darius and I might be in danger, then Deirdre might be, too. "This is a bad idea. What if Scar Man saw you?"

She shrugs. "There's nobody around. I checked."

"You didn't notice a human bulldozer with a melted face?"

She lowers the hood and shakes out her hair. "There was nobody around, honest. And I thought we might need these." She shrugs a backpack off her shoulder, zips it open, and shows what's inside.

"Flashlights?"

"Tactical flashlights. Bright enough to blind an enemy, or pick out diamonds in the dark. Plus a set of action video cameras, so we can record us discovering the treasure. I bet we'll get a zillion hits on YouTube."

Deirdre is pumped and won't listen to reason about how dangerous it might be, searching for something so valuable. "What, it's okay for you guys to have a cool adventure, and maybe do dangerous stuff, but not for me? No way!"

To be honest, I didn't try very hard to dissuade her. So a lot of what happened later—the grisly turn of events that followed—was my fault. Deirdre wouldn't have been in harm's way if I hadn't first gotten her involved.

The trouble with the future, it's never quite what you expect, even if you're as smart as Darius Drake.

As for Darius, he can't say no to Deirdre. Fact is, he doesn't say much to her at all, at least not directly, although it's obvious he's flattered that she wants to join us.

"Okay then," she says, eyes gleaming. "Where do we start? Attic? Basement? Inside the walls? Have you located any secret compartments or passageways?"

As she awaits instructions, she clips a thumb-sized camera unit to her baseball cap and sets it firmly on her head.

"We are still in the thinking-about-it stage," Darius

concedes. "I was about to list known facts and then proceed to the inductive reasoning."

"What?"

"Have a seat, this could take a while," I suggest. "You want half a candy bar?"

She settles on the old sofa and shakes her head. "Go ahead, I'm all ears."

Not even slightly true. Her ears, like everything else about her, are pretty much perfect.

Darius flips open a notebook. I haven't mentioned it before, but he doesn't have a permanent cell phone or a tablet or anything electronic, outside of the old desktop computer in his lab. Excuse me, his room. Probably because he's a Stonehill kid, and doesn't have anyone to buy him stuff like that. Not that it seems to have slowed him down any, in terms of brainpower.

"This house isn't equipped with a chalkboard," he says, "so here goes."

Using a felt-tip marker, he inscribes the following onto the peeling wallpaper between the bookshelves.

1. **Dunbar purchased a famously expensive necklace for Lucy Dare.**

2. **Lucy Dare died before he could give it to her.**

3. **Dunbar, who had been a celebrity, became a recluse and died in obscurity.**

4. **After Dunbar's death, the necklace was nowhere to be found.**

5. **The location of Lucy Dare's grave is unknown, as is Dunbar's.**

Deirdre raises her hand before he's done. "Won't you get in trouble for writing on the walls?"

"The walls belong to me, or will eventually, so I gave myself permission. Okay? Let us proceed. These five facts are not in dispute," he says, gesturing at the wall. "For decades treasure hunters have made the connection between facts four and five, and concluded that their final resting place was kept secret because that's where the diamonds are located. Grave robbers have been stealing from the dead since at least the time of the pyramids—Donald Dunbar would have been aware of that and taken precautions." Darius pushes up his glasses, glancing from me to Deirdre. "You follow?"

"Go on," Deirdre urges.

"All of which brings us to a dead end, no pun intended. That's everything we know about the case for certain. To go any further we must use facts and observations to induce possible directions and outcomes."

Deirdre raises her hand again. "You mean make educated guesses?"

Darius looks disappointed. "If you must simplify, yes. I'll go first. In regard to fact three: Dunbar became a recluse, ignoring his business until, ultimately, it failed. Contemporary accounts, mostly newspaper articles, indicate that Dunbar became quite morbid. He seems to have been obsessed with memorializing Lucy, and yet he left behind no visible monuments. From these facts, I induce that whatever memorial or monument he made for Lucy Dare is underground, out of sight. That's what all the tomb raiders assumed, and I agree."

"But they never found anything."

He nods. "As I said before, looking in the wrong place. Lucy Dare can't have been buried in a cemetery, because it would have been discovered by now. So ask yourself, if Donald Dunbar wanted to build a secret monument, a hidden tomb for his beloved, how would he do it? Who would he turn to?"

"Of course," I say, with a mental snap of my fingers. "James Rutgers."

"Exactly."

"Wait," says Deirdre. "Who is James Rutgers?"

"Donald Dunbar's closest friend, and also the man who helped him build the mills and factories. By all accounts

Rutgers was a brilliant mechanical engineer. He built something else, too. Something that may tell us where Lucy Dare is buried."

"Don't be a tease," Deirdre says. "What?"

"This house. All we have to do is unlock its secrets."

CHAPTER TWENTY-SEVEN

The Search Begins

IT'S AMAZING HOW much Darius reminds me of a teacher, the way he gestures with his felt-tip marker and rubs his chin while thinking out loud. If he doesn't become a world-famous detective I can see him as a professor. But that's in the future, and like I said, the future doesn't care what we think. It just keeps happening, whether we like it or not.

"We know from the land records and building permits that James Rutgers personally oversaw the construction of this house. That's the reason it's still standing after years of neglect. The foundation is factory-grade poured concrete. The framing is longleaf yellow pine, super-strong and highly resistant to rot. The electrical wiring and plumbing were also factory grade for their time. He spared no expense, cut no corners."

Deirdre's hand pops up. "Is this really your house?"

"Legally, yes. I can take possession when I turn eighteen."

She looks around with a calculating eye. "It needs a total makeover, but it could be cute."

"If you say so," Darius says.

"And the man who built it was best friends with Mr. Dunbar? And your grandfather searched it top to bottom for a clue to where the diamonds might be located?"

"He did, yes. And when he found nothing, this is where he 'discovered' the forged document indicating that Lucy Dare's tomb had been constructed on the grounds of Donald Dunbar's estate. Which was razed in the 1970s and eventually developed into the Dunbar Acres subdivision."

"That's where Arthur lives!"

"He does. Along with about three hundred other households. According to my grandfather's theory—based on a lot of wild speculation, in my opinion—one of the new houses had been built directly over Lucy Dare's tomb. He used money he swindled from Jasper Jones, purchased the house, tore it down, and started to dig. They hired backhoes and Bobcats and big drills, and they dug until they reached bedrock. No tomb. No nothing."

"Wow. He wrecked a house for nothing."

"A house, his reputation, and his life. All because he was convinced that Dunbar built the tomb on his own property. But that wasn't Donald Dunbar's only property. He owned the factories."

"And his best friend built a house on factory grounds," I point out.

"Exactly!" Darius says, giving me a nod of approval. "And this, we induce, was no coincidence. If I'm correct, the house had a dual purpose. It was James Rutgers's home, and it was also somehow connected to Lucy Dare's tomb. A tunnel, a door, a secret passageway? I'm not sure. But something physical. Something real. And something very cleverly hidden by a master millwright. Clever enough to have fooled the world for almost a hundred years."

"This is so cool," Deirdre says, standing up and adjusting her cap. She opens her backpack. "Flashlight, anyone?"

———

And so the search begins. We start on the main floor, poking around the bookcases for hidden switches or levers. Which means we have to unload all the books and stack them on the floor. And then put them all back when we don't find anything.

"Had to be done," Darius says, panting. "Just because a bookcase is an obvious place to hide a panel, that doesn't mean we can exclude it."

Next we crawl around inside the kitchen cupboards, looking for trapdoors. To be honest, Darius and Deirdre do the crawling because I'm too big to squeeze into the cabinets.

No luck.

Darius points to the ceiling. "Upstairs," is all he says.

So we trundle up the narrow, squeaky stairway to a dim hallway on the second floor. There are three paneled wooden doors in the hallway, one for each small bedroom.

The first is entirely empty. No furniture, no shelves of any kind. Just one narrow window overlooking the street below. Deirdre brings up a small hammer she found in a kitchen drawer and starts tapping the walls for hollow spaces. Darius and I check for loose floorboards, hidden levers, or switches.

Nothing.

Deirdre sighs. "I guess we better try door number two."

The second bedroom is far from empty. A single, iron-framed bed shoved up against the wall, the bedding neatly made. The oak desk in the corner is covered with a layer of dust. On a shelf above it, several books about Donald Dunbar and the mystery of the missing diamonds.

One of the books, a slim volume, is about Lucy Dare. Deirdre carries it to the window, where the light is better, and leafs through the book. "Wow," she says. "I had no idea how beautiful she was."

Inside the title page is a formal portrait of young Miss Dare, gazing with large, intelligent eyes directly into the camera. A hint of laughter in her smile, as if she's amused to be looking so grown-up. But the picture that really brings her to life is a group photo taken with her fellow orphans at the Stonehill Home for Children, in 1916, when she was seventeen years old. The downstairs foyer of the home is still recognizable, although everything looked much newer then. The residents, as they were then called, are dressed in their Sunday best, faces gleaming, hair neatly brushed. In the center, arms linked to the other children, stands Lucy Dare, about to "graduate" from the home into adult life, according to the caption.

You might think that would be scary, going out into the world on your own, but not to Lucy. She seems to glow with good humor and, well, just *goodness*. Even in the old photograph, her personality fills the room with warmth and kindness. Clearly the other, younger children love her as they would a sister or a mother.

The biggest part of the slim book is Lucy's prize-winning essay, written at the age of fifteen. "Why We Must Help One Another."

"If you just told me about her, I'd think she was too good to be true," Deirdre says. "Until I saw this picture. You can tell there's nothing fake about her. She really and truly believes we must help one another. At the same time, you know—I mean, look at her expression—you can tell she likes to hear a good joke. She loves to laugh! Oh, I wish I'd known her!"

"May I?" Darius says, holding out his hand.

"Sure." Deirdre gives him the book.

Darius flips back to the title page and squints through his thick glasses. "Just as I thought," he says. "A privately printed edition, compiled by Donald Dunbar, in 1920. He was memorializing her."

Which makes a light go on in my brain. I clear my throat. "Maybe a clue? Where the tomb is located?"

Darius thrusts his hand in the air. "Excellent idea, Bash Man! I shall devour each page, in search of clues."

For a moment I'm worried he might actually devour the book. Tear out the pages and eat them. Instead he pulls a chair over to the window and begins to turn the pages, his eyes locked into focus. Tuning out the world while he reads the contents, flipping the pages methodically.

"Might as well keep searching," I say to Deirdre. "He's a fast reader, but not *that* fast."

We go back into the hall. Deirdre slips ahead of me with a gleeful look and turns the knob on the third door. It creaks open into darkness. The windows of the last bedroom have been boarded up, making it difficult to see. The shadowy shapes inside could be furniture draped with dust covers.

"There must be a light," Deirdre says. "The house is wired for electricity, right?"

I fumble around the doorjamb and locate an old-fashioned switch, one you have to turn instead of flip.

A bare lightbulb comes on, blinding us for a moment. Then, as the flash of brightness fades from our eyes, Deirdre screams. Actually we both do.

There's a body hanging from a rope, and it looks like Darius Drake.

CHAPTER TWENTY-EIGHT

All for One

"IT'S CALLED AN effigy," Darius says, examining the horrible thing that hangs from the bedroom light fixture. "Stuff some old clothing with newspaper, like a dummy, and draw a face on an old soccer ball for a head, and there you have it, an effigy. Variations of this sort of thing have been going on since at least Roman times. Sometimes the effigies are burned, usually by an angry mob, sometimes they are symbolically hung as part of a protest."

"Dude, it has a red wig."

Darius folds his arms across his skinny chest. "I don't think it looks anything like me."

"They drew glasses on the face," Deirdre points out. "Black, thick frames. Just like yours."

"I didn't say it wasn't supposed to be me. Just that the resemblance is minimal. For example, I don't have a round face. I don't have a nose like a pig snout."

I say, "Dude, how come you're not freaked out? Somebody made a what-do-you-call-it, this dummy thing, and hung it from the ceiling with a sign around your neck."

"*Effigy*, from the Latin 'to shape or fashion.' And it's not *my* neck."

"You know what I mean."

Crudely printed in red Magic Marker, the cardboard placard reads:

THOU SHALT NOT STEAL

"A message, obviously. That is, don't steal the Dunbar diamonds."

"I know this is terrible and scary," Deirdre says, taking a picture with her cell phone. "But it's also sort of cool."

"Are you cracked?" I shout. "It's supposed to be Darius!"

"I said it was terrible and scary," she says, a little defensively. "But we were looking for clues, and this is a big fat clue."

"Not fat," Darius points out.

"You know what I mean. So, who did it? Who went to all the trouble to try and scare us out of the house?"

Darius pushes his glasses back up his nose and thinks about it. "Two possibilities. Jasper Jones, according to my grandfather. Or Scar Man, who keeps warning us not to search for the treasure. Supposedly because he believes we're in danger, but possibly because he already knows where the diamonds are and doesn't want us to find them. He was in the house when we arrived, and we know he has a key, so he had ample opportunity. He may have been the one who sent me the original message, written in blood. This time the message is in red Magic Marker, but it might as well be in blood."

"I hate to even bring it up, but what about your grand-father himself?" I ask. "He's the one who keeps telling you to leave the diamonds alone."

"Since he can't walk, I don't think he could manage this. Unless he was faking with the crutches."

Deirdre makes a face. "You can cross Jasper off the list. No way he would do such a thing."

"People aren't always what they seem," Darius reminds her.

Which gives me an idea. "What about Mr. Robertson? He's an expert in the life of Donald Dunbar and knows a lot about the diamonds."

"Are you serious?" Darius asks.

"You said people aren't always what they seem, right?"

"Fine," says Darius, nodding in agreement. "Add him to the list."

Staring at the effigy, Deirdre says, "Whoever did it, it seems like we've got a big decision. Should we call the police?"

"Absolutely not!" Darius responds instantly. "No way. At the very least they'll send us home."

"But this is a crime, right? Making a threat?"

Darius tries to shrug it off. "Maybe, maybe not. If this was part of a protest, it would be protected speech. And I'm pretty sure I'd have to be the one to bring charges. Which I won't."

"Why not?" I ask, looking forlornly at the scary-looking effigy.

Darius is defiant. "Because we're going to find the Dunbar diamonds. The three of us together, or me alone, if need be."

CHAPTER TWENTY-NINE

If We Scream for Help

OKAY, YOU'RE RIGHT, we should have called the cops. I get that now. But there's no stopping Darius Drake when he's on a case. It's like trying to stop the sun from coming up. And Deirdre is totally geeked about the treasure hunt. I doubt she's ever really been afraid of anything in her whole life. I mean, she thought the effigy was cool, right? Me, it's all I could do not to toss my cookies when I first saw that thing. Not that I'd had any cookies, but you know what I mean. Right now I've got a nervous stomach. Eating usually calms it down, but not today.

What happens is, Darius unhooks his effigy from the light fixture and tosses it aside like it's nothing more than a bundle of laundry, which basically it is. "Warning noted," he says dismissively. "I have no intention of stealing anything. If we locate the diamonds we'll follow the letter of the law, agreed?"

We all agree and then we get back to work, searching every dusty inch of the second floor. Darius doesn't know exactly what we're looking for, but he'll recognize it when he sees it. "Think about deception," he says. "An extraordinary thing disguised to look ordinary. Hiding in plain sight."

"Like the entrance to a secret tunnel disguised as a fireplace," Deirdre suggests.

"That's the idea."

"But there aren't any fireplaces," I point out.

"It's a concept," Darius explains. "Go with the flow, Bash Man."

The flow means checking every floorboard, every light switch, every knob and handle. Looking for something, anything, that will lead us to the treasure.

What do we find on the second floor besides the weird effigy thing? Nothing but dust. Sneezy, boring dust.

"I never said this would be easy," Darius says as we take a short break. "My grandfather searched this place for weeks and didn't find anything."

"Maybe because there's nothing here," I say grumpily.

"So you're giving up?"

"I didn't say that."

Deirdre dusts off her hands. "I'll bet there are spiders in the attic. Spiders as big as cats." She looks pleased at the idea.

"To the attic, then," says Darius, nodding in agreement.

We troop up the steep narrow stairway and open the creaky door. I'm expecting another surprise to leap out of the dimness, or swing from the roof rafters, but nothing does.

It's just an attic.

There are a few spiders, but nothing bigger than the fingernail on my smallest finger. And lots of cobwebs that are not quite transparent in the glare of our flashlights. And more sneezy, boring dust.

Other than that, the attic is wide-open and completely empty.

Not that it stops Darius from searching. He pokes and prods the creaky floorboards, pushes and pulls every rafter, inspects along the edges where the roof meets the floor, and covers every last inch of the place.

Nothing. Nada. Zippo.

There's only one more place to search.

"We've been saving the best for last," Darius announces. "I can't promise giant spiders in the basement, but at the very least there should be some interesting mold."

Deirdre brightens at the idea. "Cool," she says. "I was hoping we'd have a chance to use these."

From out of the backpack she produces three small walkie-talkies, hands them around, and gives Darius a challenging grin. "This way if we get separated and scream for help, you'll hear us."

CHAPTER THIRTY

When Something Astonishing Happens

To be honest, basements and cellars spook me out. Anything underground gives me the creeps, okay? Worms and moles, that's who belongs underground. But I don't want to look like a weenie so I follow Darius and Deirdre down the basement steps even though it makes my stomach hurt. And no, it's not because I'm hungry. The opposite. Doubt I could eat a cupcake even if it jumped into my mouth.

Unlike the attic, the basement is loaded with junk. Jam-packed. Busted furniture, empty flowerpots and gardening tools, a table with a missing leg propped on a stack of moldering books. Dozens of cans of old paint and rusty tools and at least a hundred jars of screws and washers. Piles of saggy cardboard boxes crammed with clothing and shoes and boots and stuff. In the back corner there's a stack of broken furniture, as if the owner couldn't bear to throw anything away, no matter how useless. In another corner a collection of old appliances, including an ancient stove, a treadle sewing machine, an icebox with the doors removed, and some clunky old contraption with a tub and a brass handle. Along part of the back wall are precarious stacks of crates that contain files and folders from when Winston Brooks was searching for the Dunbar diamonds. A search that led him to this very house, which is starting to look like yet another dead end.

Darius starts pulling old file folders from the crates.

"Take this," Deirdre says, handing me a chunk of iron pipe. "Keep tapping and listen for anything hollow."

We push through all the broken furniture and junk and work the outer edges, tapping on the foundation walls, Deirdre with her small hammer and me with the piece of pipe. Poured concrete, as Darius pointed out. The surface is hard and smooth, and there's no way to conceal a door or entryway without us finding it, either by spotting a seam or by locating a hollow spot.

Meanwhile Darius keeps puttering around with the crates of moldy files, squinting in the dimness as he looks for clues. Reluctantly he closes the last file box and asks, "You guys find anything?"

"Piles of stinky junk. Enough to fill ten Dumpsters."

"The foundation walls?"

Tap tap.

"Solid concrete."

Tap tap.

"Keep looking! If James Rutgers built a secret passageway, it will be very, very clever. You'll be looking right at it but you won't see it."

"It's not in the walls, that's for sure," Deirdre says, laying down her little hammer.

Darius looks up at the dangling lightbulb. "That's the only source of light, one fifteen-watt bulb?"

"That and our flashlights."

"Hmmm. The electrical wiring in the rest of the house is more than adequate, even by modern standards," Darius says. "So why is it so dim in the basement?"

I say, "Maybe whatever we're looking for is hiding in the shadows. In plain sight but, you know, hard to see. The dim light is on purpose."

He looks pleased. "Excellently induced, Bash Man. Your theory is plausible."

Inspired, Deirdre aims her powerful flashlight into the dim corners, bathing them with a bright, sweeping light. "Look! Did you see that? It gleams."

Darius peers around the stacks of file boxes. "Hold the beam steady, please."

Her flashlight illuminates the old tub with the big brass handle, partially obscured by the old icebox.

"What is that thing?" Darius wants to know.

"Wait," says Deirdre, pushing through the stacks of

junk, working her way closer. "Right, that's what I thought. An old washing machine. Probably as old as the house. That thing at the top? That's called a mangle, and you crank it by hand. The clothes went in the tub below, you added hot water that had been heated on a stove, then scrubbed the clothes on the scrub board, see, and finally you fed each item through the mangle to squeeze out the water. Took all day to do the laundry."

Darius sounds incredulous. "How do you know that?"

"An American history course. Did you know that in the old days, before modern appliances, women used to spend more than sixty hours a week doing housework and preparing meals?"

Darius sighs. "So it's just an old washing machine. Probably too heavy to carry out of the basement. Not exactly an entrance to a secret passageway."

"No," says Deirdre, getting close enough to the old machine to shine her light inside it. "But it makes me wonder, what was a man like James Rutgers doing with a washing machine?"

"Explain," Darius urges.

"He was a bachelor, right? Married to his job. I very much doubt that any man of his position—the senior millwright in one of the world's largest factories—was doing his own laundry. He'd have sent it out to be professionally laundered."

"Maybe. Or maybe he liked to do it himself."

Deirdre laughs. "Are you serious? Have you ever done laundry by hand?" She pauses. "That's what I thought. No, this machine doesn't belong here."

I get busy, shoving crates and busted furniture around to make room so we can really look at the thing. When the area around the old washing machine is clear, I shine my flashlight along the floor under it. "No idea who used the thing, but it must belong here," I say. "The legs are bolted into the concrete floor above a drain. Sorry, Deirdre, but it's just another piece of junk, that's all."

"I guess you're right," she says, disappointed.

I start to stack the crates back in place.

"Wait!" Darius says. "Hiding in plain sight, remember? You said that, Bash Man. We're looking right at it but we don't see it."

"Sorry, but all I see is a stinky old machine."

"Look again," he urges. "You see an old washing machine. I see a very clever piece of engineering."

He reaches out, gripping one of the little levers above the tub. There's a satisfying *clunk!* as it slips into place. He examines the mechanism that turns the tub, then carefully engages another lever, this time in the opposite direction.

"That should do it, if my theory is correct. Deirdre, you noticed this old thing, so you get the honors. Try turning the handle on that cranking mechanism."

She does, and something astonishing happens.

CHAPTER THIRTY-ONE

What Lies Beyond

As Deirdre cranks the big brass handle with both hands, the old washing machine slowly but surely lifts up from the floor and begins to swing to one side. Underneath the machine is a large drain grate. Darius falls to his knees, hooks his skinny fingers in the heavy grate, and drags it out of the way.

"Flashlight!"

I aim the flashlight into the exposed hole beneath the grate—easily big enough for a person, even one as wide as me—and see the glint of a curved iron staircase descending into the darkness below.

"That's it!" Darius cries out. "We did it! We found the secret passage!"

Looking back on it, we should have told someone we were about to explore a tunnel under the house on Rutgers Road. But we don't. We're so excited by our discovery that we grab our flashlights and clamber down the narrow, curving stairway into the tunnel below.

Me first, then Deirdre, then Darius.

Thirteen steps bring us to a smooth concrete floor, and into air so stale and dank it's as if no one has breathed it in a hundred years. Ahead of us a tunnel, invisible in the overwhelming darkness, leads to who-knows-where.

"What do we do now?" Deirdre whispers.

Something about the place makes us all whisper. Maybe because we're nervous about not knowing what happens next. Or maybe because when it comes right down to it, we don't want to disturb the dead.

Darius decides it's a teaching moment. "Bash Man, given what we observed about the level of construction in the house itself, what logical induction might we make about the construction of this tunnel?"

I think about it for a moment. "That it's pretty much the same?"

"Exactly!" he says, delighted at my response. "Stay where you are," he cautions us. "This will only take a minute, if my theory is correct."

He moves to the side of the tunnel and begins to run his hands along the wall. "Just as I thought. Ready, Deirdre?"

"Ready."

"Ready, Bash Man?"

"I guess."

"Here goes," Darius says, flipping a switch. "Let there be light!"

It begins as a faint glow, and then one by one a long string of overhead lightbulbs blink into life, illuminating a concrete-lined tunnel that seems to end, far in the distance, in a blank wall.

The lightbulbs are so old they could have been made by Thomas Edison, but they still function.

"Wow," says Deirdre, marveling at the string of lights. "This is so cool."

"It ends in a blank wall," I point out. "Maybe they never finished the project."

"Only one way to find out," says Darius, leading the way.

Turns out the blank wall is an optical illusion, caused by the play of shadows. The tunnel doesn't end in a blank wall, it turns ninety degrees to the right. Darius locates another ancient light switch, and the next leg of the tunnel is illuminated. Which once again looks like it ends in a blank wall.

Except it doesn't. Tucked into the final corner is a black iron door with no handle, and no obvious hinges.

This is it, the door to a tomb.

Nobody says anything. It's as if all along we've been concentrating on finding the diamonds, and now that we're nearly there, we're suddenly thinking about what it means to enter such a place. What it will likely contain, treasure or no treasure: coffins, bones, skeletons, remains of the dead.

Do we really want to go there?

Deirdre grimly plays her flashlight over the door, revealing some sort of bronze insignia brazed into the iron plating. The shape of a heart enclosing three sets of letters.

Deirdre sighs and says, "Lucy Dare and Donald Dunbar, rest in peace."

CHAPTER THIRTY-TWO

The Heart Is a Good Place to Start

WHEN I WAS little there used to be this deliciously scary show I really liked, *Tales from the Crypt,* even though it scared the poo out of me. Well, not really, but you know what I mean. Each episode was introduced by the Crypt Keeper, a ghoul who popped up from a coffin with a screaming laugh. For a long time I thought the Crypt Keeper was real, even if the stories were made up, but when I got a little older it became obvious it was only a puppet.

Which is why to this day I'm scared of puppets. And skeletons and coffins and crypts.

"Maybe we ought to think about this," I say, glancing uneasily at the black iron door.

Darius points a flashlight in my face, as if to say, *Just checking.* "Really? You think it might be booby-trapped?"

"No. I don't know, maybe. It's more like, this is a grave, right? A final resting place?"

"We won't know for sure until we open the door."

"What about 'rest in peace'?"

Darius snorts. "I'm more worried about resting in pieces."

Deirdre taps me on the arm. "You're sweet, Arthur. You're concerned about being respectful. But we've come this far. We have to find out."

"Right," I say. "You're right. So how do we open the door?"

"It's a puzzle," Darius declares. "We just have to solve it."

We all stare at the black door, as if waiting for something to be revealed. But what? "I don't get it," I admit. "There's no handle or knob or latch. No keyhole even if we had a key."

"Deirdre?"

"Sorry, Darius. I'm just not seeing a way in. I think we need a big crowbar."

"Let's think about this," he suggests. "We know from contemporary accounts that Donald Dunbar was obsessed with building a memorial for Lucy Dare. We know from our discovery that his friend James Rutgers helped him build that memorial, and that the entrance to it was hidden in the basement."

"So?"

"So, why make a secret entrance if you don't intend to use it? Why not completely seal it off? That would ensure the crypt—or whatever it is—would remain undisturbed, possibly forever. A secret entrance suggests that Dunbar used it, probably more than once, and possibly much more frequently. Paying his respects, as you would at an ordinary cemetery. If that's true, then there has to be a simple way to open this door. Hidden but simple."

"I'm still thinking crowbar," Deirdre says brightly.

"It may come to that," Darius admits.

"What about the heart?" I wonder. "The initials inside? Could it be a clue? I mean, we're assuming LD plus DD plus RIP stands for Lucy Dare, Donald Dunbar, and 'rest in peace.' But what if it means something else?"

Darius tips his head to one side, considering the question. "Like what?" he asks.

"Haven't got a clue. Thinking out loud."

Darius brightens. "Maybe not a bad thought, Bash Man. The heart is a good place to start. The center of the door, the center of Dunbar's life. It may well have more than one meaning, more than one purpose. Deirdre, could you lend me your hammer?"

She reaches into her backpack, hands him the small hammer.

Darius starts tapping around the edges of the door. It sounds solid enough, and so heavy I doubt a crowbar would scratch it. As he gets closer to the center—closer to the heart—the tone rises. Not a lot, but enough to notice.

Darius looks at us with a gleeful expression. "There's something inside the door panel. Hear that?" He taps with the hammer.

Tap. Tap. Clunk.

"Could be some sort of mechanism," he says. "A locking mechanism? If so, how is it triggered?"

Darius puts down the hammer and uses his flashlight beam to light the area where the initials have been brazed into the iron door. He puts his face close to the surface, examining it from one side, then the other. Almost mashing his glasses he's so close.

I'm thinking he needs a magnifying glass.

He stands back, wrinkling his nose as he squints.

"I put the odds of my being correct at about fifty-fifty," he says, not sounding all that confident.

"Correct about what, exactly?" Deirdre wants to know.

"This," he says, putting one thumb on Donald Dunbar's initials, the other on Lucy Dare's.

He pushes.

There are two metallic clicks as the initials sink into the iron surface, and then with a sigh, the heavy door swings open.

CHAPTER THIRTY-THREE

What the Cat Dragged In

OKAY, I'LL ADMIT it. My knees are shaking as the iron door swings wide, revealing impenetrable darkness beyond. I'm afraid to raise my flashlight, terrified of what it might reveal. Crawling spiders, grinning skulls, bony knuckles reaching from the grave. Stuff so scary I can't bear to think about it.

Deirdre grabs my arm and whispers, "What now?" in a quavering voice.

So I'm not the only one who's afraid of the dark.

Meanwhile Darius must have slipped past us somehow, because a few moments later he finds a light switch on the wall and flicks it on. Not a string of bare overhead lightbulbs this time, but something much more exotic. Something marvelous and melancholy and mysterious.

We're inside an underground chapel with an elegantly domed ceiling dotted with faintly luminous stars. The lighting is soft and low and indirect, like something you'd find in a movie theater or a museum. The gently curved walls are divided into panels by fluted Greek columns, and each panel is a painting of a shimmering lake at twilight.

It's as if we're on an island, surrounded by calm waters. And in the center of the island, raised on a marble plinth, are a pair of marble coffins with life-sized figures carved on the lids.

A male figure and a female figure, lying side by side.

"Not coffins," Darius says confidently, in full lecture mode. "Sarcophagi. Commonly used by the Egyptians, and later the Greeks, to inter their dead. Common in this country well into the twentieth century. Obviously Mr. Dunbar spared no expense."

"It's so beautiful," Deirdre says. "And so sad."

"Promise me we're not going to pry those open," I say, pleading.

Darius gives me a look that is part amused, part triumphant. "We don't have to. It looks like Donald Dunbar anticipated that someone might eventually find their resting place, and prepared accordingly."

He approaches the center of the chapel, within touching distance of the carved figures on the lids of the sarcophagi, the marble coffin things. He turns to the female figure and seems to focus on the pale marble face.

"Check this out," he says, beckoning us over.

Flashlight at her side, Deirdre edges closer. And then my sister lets out a little shriek. A shriek not of fear, but of wonder.

"Oh my," she says, at a loss for more powerful words. "Oh my oh my oh my."

My first thought is maybe there's something gross or disgusting. Bones showing through the marble, something like that. But that's impossible, and besides, Deirdre and Darius don't sound grossed out. Quite the opposite.

They make room for me, and then I see it for myself. The carved figure of the woman—an image of Lucy Dare, recognizable from her photographs—has been decorated with an astonishing jeweled necklace, lying in a shallow groove carved around the figure's neck.

The Dunbar diamonds, missing for a hundred years, are missing no more.

In addition to the necklace, the figure of Lucy Dare holds a carved tablet in her marble hands. Deirdre reads it in a voice hushed with reverence.

"Take this gift of love if you must, and do good if you can, but please leave us in peace."

Deirdre adjusts her camera-equipped baseball cap and holds the fabulous necklace up to the soft lights. It glistens like a small, perfectly contained waterfall, each diamond a drop of water filled with its own individual source of illumination. The whole thing reflects on the dome of the chapel, diamond facets transformed into a thousand beams of light.

It's impossible to believe that a thing of such beauty could be cursed. But it makes me understand why so many treasure hunters wasted so much time and dug so many holes, from the original tomb raiders in the 1930s to Winston Brooks, who tore down an entire house, all of them searching in vain for what my sister now holds in her hands.

"I have an idea," she says, lowering the necklace.

"No, you can't keep it," Darius teases.

"Not that. No, never! Their last request was to 'do good if you can,' and that's what we have to do. Part of doing good is to honor the final part of that request: Leave them in peace. Go away from this place and lock the door and never breathe a word about the secret tunnel or the chapel or what it contains. You can say you found the necklace hidden in the house, or buried somewhere else, but please don't let this become a tourist attraction."

"Charge admission? I hadn't thought of that."

"Darius!"

"I'm kidding. Actually, I agree. It was never my plan to publicize the grave site, if we managed to find it. As a matter of fact, I already have an alternate location for the discovery."

"Where do you have in mind?"

He's about to tell us when the door swings open and

Scar Man lurches into the chapel, big as murder. The soft lighting almost erases the melted part of his face, which is kind of weird, but the strangest thing is that the big man has his hands behind his back, as if he's hiding something. It looks wrong somehow, and I've almost figured out why when a smiling face peeks around from behind, partially hidden by Scar Man's bulk.

"Hello, boys and girls," Jasper Jones says, showing us his shiny pistol. "Look what the cat dragged in!"

CHAPTER THIRTY-FOUR

What's in Your Pocket?

"THIS KNUCKLE DRAGGER was skulking around your secret tunnel. Told me he was 'keeping an eye on the kids.' I'll just bet he was. Waiting for his chance to steal the diamonds right out from under you, Darius. That's what he had in mind. I warned you about that, remember?"

The sudden intrusion is so startling that it takes me a moment to notice that Scar Man has a gag in his mouth, and his hands are bound with oversized zip ties. The big man is in Jasper Jones's custody, no doubt about it. And he's blinking furiously and grimacing behind the gag, as if he has something important to tell us.

Meanwhile Mr. Jones moves with a physical strength I never noticed at the tennis club. He forces Scar Man to his knees and whips a black plastic zip tie around his ankles, rendering the big man immobile. Just like cops do on TV.

Does this mean he's a cop? Maybe working undercover? Was the whole Jack-Sparrow-at-the-tennis-club thing a disguise?

Jones, smiling grimly, slips the gleaming pistol into his waistband.

"You're lucky to be alive," he says. "Recovering the Dunbar diamonds? Very dangerous. Impressive, but dangerous."

Darius looks at Scar Man on the floor, made silent by the gag, and then up at Mr. Jones. "What if he's telling the truth?" he asks. "What if he was just keeping an eye on us?"

"Don't be naive. He's a villain. Just look at him. Look at his face."

"That was a childhood accident. You can't judge him by the scars on his face."

Jones shrugs. "You're right. Maybe I'm being unfair. It isn't the scars, it's how he behaves. That's what makes him a villain." He reaches into a pocket, takes out a soft velvet bag, and tosses it to Darius. "I better take custody of the necklace," he says. "I'll put it in my office vault, make sure it's safe until we sort this out."

Deirdre starts to hand over the necklace, but Darius stops her. "I think not," he says, looking defiant.

"What's the matter, Darius?" Jones asks. "This thug is working for your grandfather, or maybe for himself.

Whoever employs him, he wanted to get his hands on the Dunbar diamonds. I stopped him. You should be grateful."

Scar Man squirms, blinking his eyes desperately.

"Thanks," says Darius. "But we can take it from here."

"Don't be absurd." Jones sounds hurt. "The diamonds are safe with me."

"But the boys said you didn't want them," Deirdre says, clutching the necklace as if she's changed her mind about handing it over.

"Just for safekeeping," he insists.

Scar Man thrashes at his feet, desperate to communicate something.

"See?" Jones says. "He's a violent man. If I hadn't stopped him, he'd have the diamonds, and you'd all be dead. A thug like that wouldn't leave witnesses behind."

Deirdre says, "We should call the police."

Jones nods in agreement. "Of course. After the necklace is safe. There's no signal down here anyhow. It'll have to wait until we get back to the surface. Put it in the bag, Deirdre, it's all for the best."

"After we call the police," Darius insists.

Jones's voice becomes impatient. "This is getting tiresome, you playing detective. Time to let the adults handle things you could never understand."

"What don't we understand?"

"You're playing into your grandfather's hands. He's fooling you just like he fooled me."

"Darius?" Deirdre asks, not sure who to believe.

"It's possible. He could be right about my grandfather," Darius admits. "Maybe Scar Man really was trying to steal the diamonds."

Jones looks relieved. He steps forward, holding out the velvet bag.

"Possible, but not probable," Darius says.

Jones looks puzzled. "Why not?" he asks.

"Because you had zip ties in your pocket."

CHAPTER THIRTY-FIVE

And Then Nothing

JONES LOOKS BAFFLED. "Zip ties? What does that prove?"

"It proves premeditation," Darius says. "Maybe you're in the habit of carrying a concealed weapon for personal protection, but nobody carries around zip ties unless they intend to use them."

"Really?" Mr. Jones is incredulous. "I'm trying to help, and you're focused on zip ties?"

"You told us you were no longer interested in the Dunbar diamonds. That was obviously a lie, because here you are, bag in hand, attempting to secure those very diamonds."

"I told you, just to keep them safe," Jones says, exasperated.

"Obviously you had us under surveillance," Darius says. "You saw us go down into the cellar. You saw Scar Man follow us into the tunnel. And instead of calling the police, you equipped yourself with a gun and zip ties, to restrain Scar Man and whoever else might need restraining. Because recovering the necklace was your plan all along."

Mr. Jones shakes his head and chuckles. "They were right about you, kid. Smart as a whip. But maybe not smart enough."

"Really?" Darius says. "Why not?"

"Because you're the one with the smart mouth, but I'm the one with the gun." He pulls the pistol from his waistband and waves it around.

"The necklace!" he demands. "Now!"

For a moment it's so deathly quiet I can hear the pulse pounding in my veins. Waiting for the next bad thing to happen, dreading it. There's a look in Jones's eyes that sends a jolt of ice water through my veins. He's no longer the man with the cute rescue dog and the movie-star smile. It's as if a mask has fallen away, exposing a monster behind the charming disguise.

Deirdre, trembling, slips the necklace into the velvet bag and hands it to him.

"I don't understand," she says. "You're a multimillionaire, why do you need to steal from us?"

"I'm not stealing!" he snaps. "The treasure is rightfully mine."

Eyes cast down, her face hidden by the pink baseball

cap, Deirdre backs slowly away, until she's beside me, up against the wall.

"So you're in financial trouble," Darius says quietly.

Jones laughs cynically. "You might say that. Or you might say the vultures are about to descend. Lucky for me, you're so much more clever than your grandfather."

Darius nods to himself, as if it suddenly all makes sense. "This time *you're* the defrauder," he says, coming to a conclusion. "And you got found out."

Jones shakes his head. "Not quite," he says. "I'm sorry, Deirdre. Your boyfriend is right. I've been cooking the books on my investment company for years, siphoning off a million here and a million there. But the Dunbar diamonds are going to fix all that. And I'm grateful for your help."

"So it was you all along," Darius says. "You're the one who sent me the bloody note that got this all started."

Jones chuckles. "My masterstroke," he says. "And look what it got me! A boy smart enough and determined enough to succeed where his grandfather failed. It was easy, hooking you into the hunt. Like trailing a chunk of beef in front of a bloodhound. A hunting dog can't help but follow the trail because it's in his nature."

"The threatening Father's Day card to my grandfather?"

He seems amused. "A taste of his own medicine."

"And the effigy? Was that you, too?"

Jones takes a little bow. Now that he's admitted all this, he seems to be enjoying himself. "Just a reminder," he says. "Didn't want you to run off with the treasure, if you did find it."

"Put the gun away," Darius urges him. "We'll do whatever you want, I promise."

"Can't do that," Jones says, inspecting the pistol as if he's not quite sure what to do with it. "Distasteful as it may be, I can't leave any loose ends. Nope. Gotta make a clean break, start over all fresh and new."

"Mr. Jones," says Darius, in a let's-be-reasonable tone. "Surely we can discuss this?"

"Discuss what? How exactly your grandfather betrayed me? Wait, I've got it! He knew the tomb's location all along, didn't he? And told you where to find it. That's it!"

Darius shakes his head. "No. It didn't happen that way."

Jones shrugs. "All that matters is, you did find it. Professional treasure hunters have been searching for decades, and in the end three kids solve the mystery. What a stupid world!"

"We may be kids but we're not stupid," Darius says.

Jones shakes his head, his forehead now gleaming with sweat. "No, agreed, you're quite the little genius. The four-eyed freckle monster, isn't that what they called you in school? What, you think I haven't been keeping tabs on you? Why do you think I'm on the board of that idiotic orphanage? To make sure you stayed there, where I could keep an eye on you."

"Why would you want to do that?" Darius asks, sounding genuinely surprised.

Jones shrugs. "Covering all the angles."

"What angles?"

"In case you remembered me as the face looking into the car window to make sure your parents were dead," he says. "Testimony of a three-year-old would never hold up in court, but revenge spans generations. Can't be too careful."

Darius looks like he's going to be sick. "So you did kill them."

Another shrug, as if he's admitting to nothing more consequential than being late with his homework. "Collateral damage. Remember I said your parents came to see me that night? It wasn't to beg me to help your grandfather. It was to threaten me. Your mother, that conniving little witch, she found out I was embezzling from my own fund, from my own investors. Said she'd expose me if I didn't ask the court to be merciful when it came to sentencing her dear old dad. So I did what had to be done. Spur of the moment, but it worked. Except for you. My little survivor."

"Pop Pop was right all along," Darius says, sounding both stunned and angry.

Jones chuckles. "Even a broken clock is right twice a day."

He stares at us with deadened eyes, as if we're beneath his contempt. That's when I know, an awful empty feeling in my gut, that he has no intention of letting us leave the chapel alive.

Why else would he admit to being a murderer?

I'm so afraid I can barely stand up. Afraid to do something to stop him, and afraid not to. How do you stop a man with a gun if he intends to use it?

"You don't need to do this," Darius says, pleading. "Don't make it worse. You have what you want."

Jones pats his pocket, caressing the sack of diamonds. "Almost there," he says, pleased with himself. "Just have to tie up a few loose ends. Did you really think you could simply hand them over and everything would be hunky-dory? There are legal issues."

"Legal issues?"

"The fact that the diamonds were recovered on your property. Lawyers would have a field day with that, even if you gave the treasure to me of your own free will. I'm an adult, you're a minor, they'd never buy it. Legally you would be first in line to share in the proceeds. No, the Dunbar diamonds have to be discovered on *my* property."

"That's your plan?"

"My plan is, I win, everybody else loses. Simple, really."

Darius edges a little closer. "You've got what you want. Leave us alone."

"Get back, freckle boy," Jones says, waggling the pistol. "Get down on the floor. Now!"

Darius reluctantly lowers himself to the floor, sitting cross-legged. Behind his thick glasses, his eyes are desolate. He's as scared as me. Scared because he's figured out how this will end, or maybe because he's the one who got us into this mess, or both.

My brilliant friend swallows the lump of fear in his throat and says, "You can still walk away. 'Discover' the diamonds on your own property, like you say. It would be our word against yours, and possession is nine-tenths of the law."

"Nice try. But that's just a saying. There's no such law. Believe me, I've been involved in enough lawsuits to know. If this gets into court they'd make me look like a bad guy, preying on an orphan kid, and there goes the money. I'd be ruined, and I can't have that. I have an image to maintain. Status in the community."

"The tennis club?" Deirdre says, disgusted. "You're doing this for the tennis club?"

The pistol swings in her direction. "You're sneering at me? Really?" He seems faintly repulsed at the idea. "You know the sound of fingernails on slate? That's what it sounds like to me, an adult with all my success and experience, being sneered at by a snarky teenager." He makes a claw of his gun-free hand, scrabbling it on an invisible chalkboard. "Scree scree scree!"

Satisfied with his put-down, he takes a look around the chapel tomb, as if for the first time. "Very impressive. And bigger than I expected. Which is going to come in handy. Just think of it, kids. Maybe a thousand years from now some future archaeologist will unearth this tomb. Maybe they'll think Donald Dunbar and his fiancée were some sort of divine royalty like the pharaohs, and you were underlings sacrificed to appease their gods, or protect them in the underworld. Something like that. Cool, huh?"

"Mr. Jones," Darius pleads. "Please."

Jones whirls around, aiming at my freckle-faced friend. "What? Please be quick? You want to get this over with? Okay, fine, your request is granted."

His finger tightens on the trigger.

"DON'T!" Deirdre screams.

Jones wheels on my sister, pistol fully extended. Aiming for her heart. "You're right. Ladies first."

He squeezes the trigger.

No thought involved, no brainpower required. Just a pure physical reaction that makes me leap between my sister and the gun. The first shot rips through my side like a scorching-hot iron. The second shot explodes in my face, a flash of white-hot light, and then . . .

Nothing.

CHAPTER THIRTY-SIX

TV News Ticker

BREAKING NEWS . . . IN A BIZARRE CONCLUSION TO THE HUNT FOR THE LONG-LOST DUNBAR DIAMONDS, FINANCIAL MOGUL JASPER JONES HAS BEEN ARRESTED ON MULTIPLE CHARGES THAT COULD INCLUDE MURDER IF THE VICTIM DOESN'T SURVIVE . . . JONES WAS KNOCKED UNCONSCIOUS AS HE ATTEMPTED TO EXECUTE A FOURTEEN-YEAR-OLD GIRL . . . HER STEPBROTHER INTERVENED AND WAS SHOT IN THE ABDOMEN AND HEAD AS HE COLLIDED WITH JONES, SLAMMING HIM INTO A WALL SO HARD THAT THE SUSPECT LOST CONSCIOUSNESS . . . STOMPANADO RESIDENT VINCENT MEEKS HELPED DETAIN THE SUSPECT WHILE THE POLICE WERE SUMMONED . . . THIRTEEN-YEAR-OLD ARTHUR BASH IS BEING HAILED AS A HERO . . . HE REMAINS IN INTENSIVE CARE . . . A HOSPITAL SPOKESPERSON DESCRIBES HIS CONDITION AS "TOUCH AND GO" . . .

CHAPTER THIRTY-SEVEN

Her Pink
Baseball Cap

DARK NOTHINGNESS. Distant voices. First thing that comes into focus is two faces hovering over me. A nurse and a hospital technician. Mom and Dad.

Then I fall back to sleep.

Next thing, I'm waking up again and they're still there, in the exact same places. Mom squeezes my hand. Dad says something, but I can't make out what it is because I'm falling back to sleep.

Stuff like that keeps happening. I can't seem to sort out the dream parts from the awake parts. Somebody rolls me on my side. Somebody sticks another needle in my arm. Days and nights go by, mooshed together. Eventually it smooths out and I can understand what people are saying.

MOM: "Arthur, dear, can you hear me? The infection has been stabilized. You're going to be fine."

DAD: "Son? Don't take this the wrong way, but it's a good thing you have a thick skull."

Later I found out they did three surgeries on me over five days, all under heavy anesthesia, so it's no wonder the whole experience was foggy and dreamlike. Anyhow, they fixed the bullet hole by removing a little corner of my stomach. Plenty left over, they said. Ha-ha, very funny.

Almost dying made me pretty cranky. But my dad was right, it turns out I do have a fairly thick skull. Not as thick as your average boxer, but thick enough that the second bullet skidded off the bone. Gave me a concussion, a pretty bad one, but no permanent damage.

I don't remember exactly when, but at some point Mom told me Jasper Jones had been arrested and was being held without bail, on an initial charge of attempted murder. Somehow or other I crashed into him after the shooting, and he hit his head on Dunbar's sarcophagus. Maybe the diamonds really are cursed, because he passed out. Scar Man tied him up and sat on him while Darius and Deirdre ran to call 911, police and ambulance, and led the first responders into the tunnel.

All that excitement and I missed it. If you don't count watching the video Deirdre recorded on her little GoPro camera, the one she clipped to the brim of her pink baseball cap. The one that recorded Jasper Jones bragging about running Darius's parents off the road, and him threatening all of us, and him shooting me.

Sorry, but I didn't watch that part.

CHAPTER THIRTY-EIGHT

Rumors Are Swirling

NEWS OF THE MILLS
The Dunbar Mills Blog

UPDATE—Charges against investment-fund mogul Jasper Jones have been upgraded to include second-degree murder, relating to the vehicular deaths of David and Eleanor Drake nearly ten years ago. The additional charges were brought after a disputed video file was allowed into evidence. The video was recorded by one of the underaged victims of the alleged attack. Mr. Jones's team of defense attorneys vows to appeal. If convicted of all charges, including the charges of attempted murder of three minors, Jones could be sentenced for thirty years to life in prison. Meanwhile the suspect is being held without bail, amid swirling rumors that his investment fund is being investigated, and that further charges may be in the offing.

Pending various legal decisions, it appears the infamous Dunbar diamonds will be going up for auction, with the proceeds dedicated to a scholarship fund for the children of Dunbar Mills, beginning with residents of the Stonehill Home and the Stompanado Housing Complex.

Looks like lots of local kids may soon be able to attend college free of charge. Hurray for that!

Rumors are still swirling about where, exactly, the famed necklace was recovered. Sources close to this blogger—a certain white-haired historian and author—strongly indicate the location has been sealed and will never be revealed, out of respect for the deceased.

CHAPTER THIRTY-NINE

This Mess Called Life

THE HOSPITAL FINALLY released me after eleven days. Felt like eleven months or eleven minutes, depending on my mood. I was perfectly fine to walk, but they made me ride in a wheelchair. Mom pushing, Dad walking beside me with a hand on my shoulder, chatting with me like he'd chat with a grown-up, which is weird but good.

"My suggestion is we go out the back and avoid the cameras," he says. "Your mother agrees, but it's your call."

"Back is fine. What cameras?"

He glances at me and chuckles. "You're famous, Arty. The governor has a medal to give you, as soon as you're ready, and the *Today* show wants to fly you to New York for an interview, all expenses paid."

"Seriously? Can you guys come, too?"

Dad looks uncomfortable, probably at the idea of going

anywhere with my mom, but he says, "I'm pretty sure we could work it out."

"Right now I just want to go home."

"Whatever you want," he says.

I like the sound of that. Not that I expect it to last.

There's an old black Suburban waiting for us out back, behind the Dumpsters, with Scar Man holding the door. "My wheels are your wheels," he says with a clunky, metal-toothed smile.

Right then I decide not to call him Scar Man anymore. From now on he's Mr. Meeks or Vincent, whichever he prefers.

When the Suburban finally pulls into our driveway, I notice a banner hanging from the rails on the front porch.

WELCOME HOME TO OUR HERO!

"That's embarrassing," I say.

"Better get used to it," Mom says. "You're going to hear that a lot."

Truth is, I'm really not in the mood for a welcome-home party, but there's no way to avoid it without being a total jerk. Deirdre and Darius are the first to ambush me. The red-haired freckle monster high-fives me and says, "Bash Man! Way to go!" and Deirdre doesn't say anything because she's all weepy and everything. Later she calls me "my big brother" and I say, "I'm younger than you, how can I be your big brother?" And she says, "You just are, that's how."

The man with all the names, Mystery Man, Winston Brooks, Pop Pop, he swings over on his crutches, looking way better than the last time I saw him.

"Good to be out, eh?" he says, taking a deep breath. "Amazing work you boys did. Astonishing. Darius is obviously way smarter than me, and even more bullheaded, and you're obviously way braver."

"I wish people would stop saying that. I couldn't help it. My feet made me do it."

The old treasure hunter laughs. "Whatever you say. Just wanted you to know how grateful I am for what you did. Or what your feet did, if you prefer. How you doing with all this?" he asks, glancing around at the crowd.

"Fine," I say. "I'm good."

But the truth is, I'm not sure.

There's cake and Cokes and candy bars, but for some reason I'm not hungry, which is weird. I feel the same but different. Like everything was leading up to that one moment when I had to jump or watch my sister die, and now it's over, and I'm waiting for whatever happens next.

I mutter something like that to Mr. Robertson, who isn't shy about eating cake, and he says, "That's as good a definition of being alive as any. Welcome to my world, young Mr. Bash."

Later on, Darius slides by. All during the welcome-home party he's been a combination of loud, shy, and aloof, which is typical. Partly he's not sure how to behave with his grandfather. They seem to talk, exchanging a few words, and then Darius drifts away, aloof again. Getting to know each other will take some time, obviously. He keeps breaking eye contact as he talks to me, like he's embarrassed or afraid to tell me something. "You heard I was donating the necklace?"

"Yeah. That was the right thing to do, for sure."

"If we ever need to make some money, maybe we could write a book about it. Pop Pop thinks it's a worthy concept, and Mr. Robertson said he'd help."

"Cool, dude. That's a great idea. I might even read it."

He clears his throat and sighs. "I'm really sorry about you getting hurt, Bash Man. I should have anticipated the possible intrusion by Jasper Jones, and taken precautions. He fit the parameters of our list of suspects, but I missed it. He fooled me into thinking he was a good guy, I guess."

"It's okay, Darius. We all make mistakes. My mistake was walking in front of a loaded gun . . . That's a joke."

"Yeah. Good one."

"Can I ask you a favor? Please don't call me Bash Man. Call me Arthur. Or Art."

"Or Arty Farty?"

"I'm serious."

"So am I. That hospital food gave you gas."

"Don't make me laugh. It hurts."

"Did you know an average fart is fifty-nine percent nitrogen, twenty-one percent hydrogen, nine percent carbon dioxide, four percent oxygen, and one percent sulfide gas? It's the sulfide gas that makes the stink. And Arthur? Yours is no average fart."

That does it, I'm laughing out loud at a stupid fart joke. Laughing deep and hard and long. Laughing with my goofball genius friend who dragged me into this mess called life. I look around and see Deirdre smiling at me, and my dad off to one side, looking puffed up with pride, and my mom at the kitchen counter chatting happily with Mr. Robertson and Winston Brooks, and even Mr. Meeks proudly guarding the front door, and I'm thinking this is pretty great. Family and friends and laughter and stories to tell.

What could be better?

Afterword

I first fell in love with mysteries at the Old Pagoda Dancehall and Luncheonette in Rye Beach, New Hampshire. The dance hall had been converted to summer rental apartments before I was born, but if the owner happened to be your grandmother, pan-fried hot dogs were still available at the luncheonette counter, which then served as my nana's kitchen. In addition to hot dogs and grilled cheese sandwiches, library privileges were extended. Nana was a voracious reader of mysteries, and the main room of the old dance hall housed her collection of books by Rex Stout, creator of genius detective Nero Wolfe; Agatha Christie, who dreamt up Hercule Poirot and Miss Marple; and Arthur Conan Doyle, who made Sherlock Holmes so convincing in every detail that a young reader might be forgiven for believing he was real.

We lived next door to the Pagoda and my parents often rented out our house for the summer, so on my eleventh summer I was assigned to a room above the dance hall, and it was there, under the covers with a flashlight, that I read mystery after mystery, and began to think that maybe, just possibly, I, too, might be an author when I grew up. Except I didn't wait to grow up. I started writing stories in sixth grade and somehow never stopped. For many years I published mysteries and thrillers for adult readers, until stumbling upon the idea of a tale about two outsider kids who team up for the adventure of *Freak the Mighty*.

Now it seems I've come full circle, with two outsider kids teaming up to solve a mystery. Thank you, Rex; thank you, Agatha; thank you, Arthur; thank you, Nana. Here's hoping my own effort is under-the-covers worthy.

Don't forget the flashlight!

About the Author

Newbery Honor author Rodman Philbrick has written more than a dozen award-winning novels for young readers, but before he began writing children's books, he was a prizewinning author of mysteries for adults. Two of those novels were nominated for the Shamus Award for the best detective fiction of the year, and his novel *Brothers and Sinners* won the award in 1993. His passion for the mystery genre, where he learned how to make readers turn the page, can now be found in the deliciously suspenseful *Who Killed Darius Drake?*

Mr. Philbrick's first novel for young readers, *Freak the Mighty*, has nearly four million copies in print and won the California Young Reader Medal before its release as a feature film, *The Mighty*, starring Sharon Stone. In 2009, *The Mostly True Adventures of Homer P. Figg*, about an orphan boy's adventures as he searches for his brother during the American Civil War, was chosen as a Newbery Honor Book and an ALA Notable Book among its many honors. Mr. Philbrick's other award-winning titles include *Max the Mighty, The Fire Pony, The Young Man and the*

Sea, REM World, The Last Book in the Universe, Zane and the Hurricane: A Story of Katrina, and *The Big Dark*—all published by The Blue Sky Press.

Mr. Philbrick grew up in a small town in New England, and he currently divides his time between Maine and the Florida Keys. You can learn more about him on his website: www.RodmanPhilbrick.com.